GIFTING ME TO HIS BEST FRIEND

A TOUCH OF TABOO NOVEL

KATEE ROBERT

TRINKETS AND TALES LLC

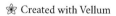 Created with Vellum

ALSO BY KATEE ROBERT

Book 2: The Fearless King

The Hidden Sins Series
Book 1: The Devil's Daughter
Book 2: The Hunting Grounds
Book 3: The Surviving Girls

The Make Me Series
Book 1: Make Me Want
Book 2: Make Me Crave
Book 3: Make Me Yours
Book 4: Make Me Need

The O'Malley Series
Book 1: The Marriage Contract
Book 2: The Wedding Pact
Book 3: An Indecent Proposal
Book 4: Forbidden Promises
Book 5: Undercover Attraction
Book 6: The Bastard's Bargain

The Hot in Hollywood Series
Book 1: Ties that Bind
Book 2: Animal Attraction

The Foolproof Love Series
Book 1: A Foolproof Love
Book 2: Fool Me Once
Book 3: A Fool for You

Out of Uniform Series

CHAPTER 1

*W*e're vacationing with Derek for the holidays, just like we do every year. A tradition that I inherited with my marriage to Grayson. Every time Christmas rolls around, it's an additional a complication I don't need, a temptation I know better than to even consider. He's my husband's best friend. Bromance doesn't begin to cover it. They're closer than brothers, close enough that I get jealous sometimes. How can I not when sometimes I catch Grayson looking at him like *that*?

I stare out the window at the pristine white mountain. Normally, we travel somewhere warm with a beach during the holidays, but Grayson's been feeling nostalgic for a "real" Christmas with snow and nature, so this year it's Colorado. He and Derek spent all day skiing, but throwing myself down a mountain and hoping for the best isn't my idea of a good time, so I bundled up here in our cabin with my e-reader and enough tea to outlast a siege.

Cabin.

The descriptor is laughable. This building, tucked as it is into the slope, is as much a cabin as our penthouse is an apartment. It's outfitted in high-end appliances, the towering vaulted ceiling is made of real logs, and all the furniture is mountain chic. It's not a beach resort, but even I can admit that it's cozy and beautiful.

And I'm doing a poor job of distracting myself.

I watch Grayson and Derek out of the corner of my eye. They couldn't be more different. Both are white but that's where the similarities end. Grayson is built lean, courtesy of his hours spent running as he trains for one marathon or another, and he's got a head of curly black hair. Derek is built bulkier with lighter brown hair and a full beard. Every time I look at him, the word that comes to mind is *thick*. Add in his penchant for wearing flannel, and he looks like a lumberjack that can rip down trees with his bare hands.

They've both showered and changed and are wearing what passes for relaxing clothing. Jeans and a knit sweater for Grayson. Lounge pants and nothing else for Derek. As if he doesn't care that the lines of his body draw a person's gaze down, down, down to the faint trail of hair leading from his navel to the drawstring of his pants.

I jerk my eyes to the window again, but the fading light turns it into a mirror, reflecting the living room back to me. I can see myself, curled on the couch with a throw blanket, and the men standing farther back in the kitchen.

"Emma?"

My skin gets hot with embarrassment, even though I haven't technically done anything wrong. "Sorry, I was mentally wandering."

Grayson comes and leans over the back of the couch to press a kiss to my temple. "Would you like a drink?"

"*Yes.*"

He chuckles at the strength of my response. "Thought so."

I give in to temptation to twist and watch him walk back to the kitchen. The first thing I noticed about him when we met seven years ago is how nicely he filled out a pair of jeans, and nothing much has changed in the intervening time. Grayson's ass is *biteable*.

Derek barks out a laugh. "You sure you want a drink? If Emma was looking at me the way she looks at you, I'd be hauling her back to our bedroom."

"You'd haul my wife back to your bedroom?" Grayson asks it mildly, and even from here I can see his lips twitch. "Fuck, Derek, tell me how you really feel."

Derek looks at me. I can't see the brown starbursts in his hazel eyes from here, but I know they're there. He's smiling like this is a joke, but there's an awareness there in the depths of his eyes. The same one that heats me up on the inside. We're attracted to each other. We have been since we met at my and Grayson's wedding. We might joke about it with my good-natured husband, but there's just enough truth for it to sting.

I wish I had a drink in my hand, because my laugh comes out a little strained. "Don't I get a say in this?"

"Definitely not." Grayson grabs a bottle of wine and pours three generous glasses. "You're my wife, which means my property. I'm pretty sure it says that in the marriage contract."

I roll my eyes. He might deliver his jokes drily enough for someone who doesn't know him to take them at face value, but they *are* jokes. Really terrible jokes. "I knew I should have read the fine print."

"Your loss, my love." He returns to the couch with two glasses of wine and sinks down next to me. "You sure you don't want to come skiing tomorrow? We can take you on the bunny hill."

I smother a sliver of disappointment that we've moved on from the conversation of passing me around. It's only ever been joking. Grayson and I get freaky in the bedroom, but adding in another person is a fantasy we've never actually followed through on. If we *did* ever go that route, doing it with his best friend would be a terrible idea.

Because I'm not the only one attracted to Derek.

I take a sip of wine and try for a smile. "I'll take a pass. There's a really cozy chair next to the fireplace with my name on it, and half a dozen books to work through while I'm on vacation." Not to mention the fifty others that are sitting unread on my e-reader. I keep meaning to stop buying new ones until my reading catches up to my purchases, but it never happens.

Derek drops into the chair across from us. He really should put on a shirt. It's distracting as hell to watch his muscles move beneath his skin as he sits forward and back. The man is all restless energy, and always has been.

He catches me looking and skates his own perusal down my body. I'm suddenly achingly aware of how my black leggings cling and the fact that I didn't bother with a bra under my slouchy sweater. Derek grins. "You two are almost a matching pair."

I glance from Grayson's sweater to mine. They're both gray, though mine is light and his is dark. "That happens after being married for a small eternity."

"Seven years last summer." Derek sips his wine, watching us with his witchy eyes. "The seven-year itch is a real thing."

I give a nervous laugh. "Right. As if you'd know with all the long-term relationships you've been in." In all the time I've known him, I haven't met a single significant other, though I know there have been a scattering of both boyfriends and girlfriends because Grayson told me.

"We're not talking about my relationships. We're talking about yours." He leans forward, expression intent. "How are you spicing things up these days?"

His willingness to ignore any and all social niceties is

something I love and hate about Derek in equal measures. I can't count on him to back off from asking questions no polite person would ask. He and Grayson are too close, too willing to share things. Neither are particularly good at boundaries.

I very carefully don't look at Grayson. "Our sex life is fine." Better than fine, really. Even after all this time, we can't get enough of each other. At least a few days a week, he stops by on his lunch break and we bang like a pair of horny newlyweds. We meet in bars and pretend to be strangers and fuck in the bathroom, in the parking lot, in the car itself. The games just get more elaborate as time goes on.

"Fine," Derek repeats slowly. He glances at Grayson, and I don't miss the fact that he gives my husband the same thorough once-over that he gave me. "That sounds depressing as hell."

Grayson laughs. "So we're back to you being jealous." He finishes his wine and sets the glass aside. Both Derek and I have most of our glasses left, but there's a new tension in Grayson that wasn't there before. I recognize it even before he looks at me. "You finished?"

There's only one answer to that question, and I'm already nodding, my body flushing hot in anticipation. "Yes." I set my glass aside and take his hand as he rises. He moves quickly, scooping me up and tossing me over his shoulder. My exhale whooshes out in a breathless laugh. "Grayson!"

"If you'll excuse us, I'm going to go have *fine* sex with my gorgeous wife."

"Well, fuck you, too." Derek laughs. "Have fun, kids. I'll be in my room with my hand to keep my company."

I catch sight of him through the long fall of my blond hair as Grayson hauls me away, watching us with a visceral heat in his eyes. I can't tell whose ass he's most intent on, mine or my husband's. In the end, it doesn't matter. I've survived yet another conversation with him, yet another round of teasing that isn't quite teasing.

Grayson carries me into our bedroom and drops me on the bed. I barely get my hair out of my face before his mouth is on mine. It doesn't matter how many times we've done this, he kisses me like he might never get another chance. I'm already going for the front of his jeans, desperate to purge the uncomfortable thoughts, the forbidden desire that I have no business feeling. It doesn't matter where it originates, only that I slake it with my husband.

Unfortunately, that reasoning feels flimsy at best. Especially when I've fantasized about Derek more times than I care to count.

Grayson breaks the kiss long enough to pull my sweater over my head. He huffs out a laugh. "No bra."

I shake my head and grab his hand, pressing it to the apex of my thighs. "No panties, either."

He curses and goes to his knees between my legs, kissing his way down my stomach. "Tell me the truth, Emma. You finger yourself while you read those dirty books, don't you?"

He knows I do. He's caught me more than once. I gasp out a breath as he dips down and kisses my pussy through my leggings. "They're called one-handed reads for a reason."

"Mmm." He keeps kissing me there, until my leggings are soaked from his mouth and my desire. "I should send the author a thank-you note for always having my wife hot and ready for me." He finally tugs down my pants slowly, trailing kisses and licks over every bit of exposed skin. "Tell me about the one you were reading today."

Another of our games: playing out some of the dirtier scenes in my favorite books.

Except this time, I don't want to tell him. I lace my fingers through his hair and tug him back up toward my clit. "Just eat my pussy. Please."

He exhales against my clit, but he's watching me with those dark blue eyes. "You're dodging my question. Why?"

Because it's too close to home, too close to speaking the forbidden. I give his hair another tug, but he doesn't move. "Grayson, please."

His brows draw together. I have half a second to brace and then he pushes to his feet and strips out of his clothes. Even as weirdly guilty as I feel, I catch my breath at the sight of him naked. Lean and strong and a big cock just for my pleasure. I reach for him, but he catches my hand and uses his hold to flip me onto my stomach. "What—"

His weight presses against my back, pinning me in place even as he wedges his legs between mine, spreading me. Grayson slides a hand down my stomach to stroke my clit. "Tell me." He doesn't give me a chance to deny him, sliding into me in a smooth move and kissing the back of my neck. He exhales against the damp spot and my toes curl. "Indulge me, Emma. Tell me about your book."

I can't deny him, not as he starts fucking me slowly. Not when he's kissing that spot on my neck that turns me molten hot and mindless. Not with his fingers creating a delicious friction against my clit.

I gasp. "It's a ménage."

"Mmm." He keeps up his sexy assault, and it's hard to remember why I didn't want to tell him this. "Two men?"

"Yes." I moan, trying to arch back onto his cock, but he has me too effectively pinned. I am fully at his mercy, and he seems to be in no hurry. He grinds into me, rubbing my clit against his fingers with the movement of his hips, and words spill from my lips. "It's a husband and wife...and his friend. The wife and the friend fuck, a lot." I fist my hands into the comforter, my body shaking as he works me toward orgasm. "And there's this scene..." I shouldn't keep going, but I can't stop. "Her husband fingers her under a blanket while the friend is in the room. I keep going back to it because it's so hot. I touched myself to it today."

He shifts up a little until his low voice is in my ear. "Do you want me to play with that pretty pussy while my friend is sitting in the same room?"

Yes, oh god, yes I do.

CHAPTER 2

I can't catch my breath, can't figure out what answer I *should* give. In the end, I can only tell the truth. "Maybe." Maybe I *do* want Grayson to finger me under a blanket while Derek is in the room with us.

My husband keeps up that slow fucking. "It won't work. If he thinks I've got my fingers inside you while he's right there, he'll take it as an invitation." His voice goes lower yet. "Derek would rip off that blanket just so he could watch."

I can't believe he just said Derek's name while he's inside me. It doesn't matter that he's not saying it like *that*. It feels like he brought the other man into the bed with us.

I am not even remotely opposed to the idea, terrible though it is.

"Would you stop?" I whisper.

"No, baby. I wouldn't stop until you come." He shifts my legs wider and uses his hand to urge my hips up a little. The angle allows his cock to sink even deeper into me. "You're so wet. I think you like the idea of him watching."

I press my face to the comforter to avoid answering. It

doesn't seem to matter. My body is telling on me, because I *do* like the idea of Derek watching.

Grayson isn't done, though. "Maybe I'm feeling generous. Maybe I'd let him have a little touch…A little taste."

His words drive me over the edge. I come so hard I shriek, every muscle in my body going tight as pleasure cascades over me in waves, on and on, driven by the way Grayson fucks me, by the image he's created.

He follows me over the edge, holding me close. He rolls us onto our sides, his cock still inside me, and presses another kiss to the back of my neck. "You like that idea."

I can't tell what he's thinking with him behind me. His tone is dry, but it's *always* dry. Even after seven years of marriage, I sometimes need facial expression cues to know if he's being serious or joking. I try for a laugh, but it comes out forced. "I like you fucking me. You always make me come."

"Mmm." He trails his fingers up my stomach, making me squirm…and then moan when I feel him hardening again.

"Again?"

"Call me inspired." He cups my breasts, but seems content to stay seated deep inside me. The way he plays with my nipples is almost idle, distracted, and somehow that makes it even hotter.

"*Grayson.*"

"I like it, too," he says abruptly.

I freeze. "What?"

"The fantasy. Having my fingers in your pussy while he watches. Watching *his* fingers in you, his mouth on you." He hesitates. "Watching you ride his cock. I think I'd like that. I think I'd like it a lot."

I can't stop myself from clenching around my husband's cock in response to his admission, my body once again telling on me. "What are you saying?"

Grayson hooks one hand under my thigh and lifts my leg

wide to hook over his hip. He starts moving slowly, fucking me deep and thoroughly. "We play games all the time, act out fantasies. How is this any different?"

"I don't—" I gulp in a breath. "I can't think with you doing that."

"Doing what?" He starts stroking my clit again and nips the sensitive spot where my shoulder meets my neck. "Doing this?"

"Grayson, I'm serious. What are you saying?" Except I don't sound serious. I sound like I'm asking him for permission. I don't even know for *what*.

"A new game, Emma." He thrusts deep, and I can't stop myself from moaning, loud and wanton. "I want to give you to Derek. One night. I want to watch him eat your pussy, make you come, fuck you." He keeps driving my desire higher with his movements and words. "I want to wrap you up like a gift just to watch him rip the ribbons off you."

And then I'm orgasming again. My body screaming *yes, yes, yes* even as my mind is shouting of danger ahead. This time, Grayson doesn't follow me over the edge. He pulls out and shoves me onto my back, and then he's inside me again, stroking hard and deep. "Tell me you don't want it and I'll drop it."

I can't think through the pleasure, can't do more than cling to him as he stares down at me, demanding a truth I'm not sure we're ready to have between us. "You're buzzed. Lust-drunk. It's a terrible idea."

Grayson stops moving and looks down at me. There's something like vulnerability in his eyes. "Tell me the truth, Emma."

I open my mouth to lie, to send us veering back into safety, but I can't look him in the face and speak anything but the truth. Not even about this. "It sounds hot as hell," I whisper. "I could get off on being his gift alone, because *you're* the one directing it."

He starts moving again, rougher this time. "And because you get off on being bad."

"Yes." There's no use denying *that*. We have too much history of playing that particular game. I love pretending I'm doing things I shouldn't, love it when Grayson indulges me, letting me play the dirty little slut. It's always worked for us, because it's *us*.

He drives into me one last time and buries his face in my neck as he comes. I stare at the ceiling and mentally prepare for him to take it all back. Dirty talking, playing out fantasies, anything said during sex doesn't have to hold up to the light of day. We're just playing. That's all.

Except as Grayson pulls out of me and arranges himself at my side, it doesn't feel like playing. It feels like we've taken the first step down a road that could lead to the ruin of everything I hold dear in this world.

He reaches up and cups my jaw, gently guiding me to look at him. "I meant what I said."

I lick my lips. "It sounds really sexy in theory but…"

"If you don't want to do it, we won't." He doesn't move, doesn't seem to breathe. "But I think you're a hell of a better Christmas gift than the watch I got him."

"You can't mean it." When he just looks at me, I continue. "Grayson, even if I were reckless enough to say yes, this is the kind of thing that makes his visiting our house in the future weird. You'll resent me. It will *change* things."

"Emma." He presses a kiss to my forehead. "How many times have we played strangers to each other?"

I know where he's going with this, but I answer honestly. "More times than I can count."

His blue eyes are oh so serious as he studies my face.

"We've talked about you fucking a stranger while I watch almost as many times."

"Yes, a *stranger*."

"You aren't safe with a stranger, baby. That's why we've never done it. You're safe with Derek."

My body might be, but there's so many strings attached to this scenario, I'll be entangled before we ever get to actually having sex. "He's your best friend."

"Yes. And you're my wife." He brushes his thumb across my cheekbone. "You're the two people I care most about in this world."

"But—"

"Tell me you're not attracted to him." He's still holding me frozen with his direct gaze. "Tell me you haven't been eye-fucking him every time he walks around without a shirt."

"That's not fair." Not when *Grayson* does the same damn thing.

"I'm not condemning you. I'm offering you a chance to play out a fantasy we've both wanted for a long time."

I sit up. I feel too panicked to hold still, but a selfish part of me wants to say yes and damn the consequences. It's just sex, right? Derek and I have seven years' worth of pent up desire to work out on each other; surely no matter what it's like, fucking him can't hold up against what I've built up in my head.

Maybe it'll be a good thing. Get it out of the way, rip off the bandage, take away the element of the forbidden.

Or maybe I'm looking for an excuse.

I take a slow breath, trying to calm my racing heart. "How will it work?"

Grayson's eyes light up. "I'll talk to him about it tomorrow while we ski. Tomorrow night after we get back, I'll put you under that giant Christmas tree in the living room and let him unwrap you." He licks his lips. "It's Christmas Eve, so the gift lasts through Christmas."

"Is that one night or two?"

He studies me. "Two. Christmas Eve and Christmas. We leave the day after Christmas anyways."

"Right. I knew that." I give myself a shake. "What happens if it changes things?"

"We're all adults, Emma. We can handle it."

I'm not so sure he's right, but he's offering me something I've fantasized about for years. One day, two nights. What's thirty-six hours in the grand scheme of things? A small eternity and no time at all. Despite the fact that he just made me come twice, my pussy gives a pulse of need at the thought of going through with this. "Yes."

CHAPTER 3

I spend the entirety of the next day a hot mess. I can't concentrate enough to read, so I go a full pampering route, bathing and shaving and lotioning and primping until I feel moderately more in control.

And I masturbate. A lot.

Who can blame me?

In a few short hours, my husband is going to *gift* me to his best friend and then watch us fuck. It's the stuff dirty fantasies are made of, and knowing that it's going to happen only drives my chaotic desire hotter.

I'm in the middle of one such session, laying on the bed and teasing myself with slow strokes of my fingers, when Grayson walks into the bedroom. He closes the door and leans against it, raising his brows even as his gaze zeroes in to where my fingers move between my spread legs. "Getting started early?"

"I was missing you." I pull at the ties of my robe so that it will part and expose my breasts. "Come here."

He undresses slowly, layer after layer of his winter gear,

until he's standing naked before me with his cheeks still pink from the cold. "You look good enough to taste."

"Come taste me then."

He's tall enough to reach my spot on the mattress without climbing up and yanks me down toward him. "Derek's taking a shower. We don't have much time to get you ready."

My body thrills at the reminder of what's coming next. "Better hurry," I whisper.

Grayson goes to his knees beside the bed and then he kisses my pussy. His cheeks are cold and his mouth is hot and I squeak a little as he sucks on my clit. There's no teasing. He goes after me like he wants to remind me who I belong to, like he's staking his claim before handing me off to another man.

It's so fucking hot.

I sift my fingers through his hair and lift my hips to grind against his tongue. "I'm going to come too fast if you don't slow down," I gasp.

He doesn't. He just shoves me into an orgasm, fast and dirty. I'm still shaking when he lifts his head and presses a quick kiss to my mouth. "I got you something."

I reach for him. "Come here. I need you inside me."

"Nope." He gives me another kiss. "It's in the living room. Go get it while I'm in the shower and be back before I'm done."

I barely wait for him to walk into the bathroom to fix my robe and hurry out into the living room to see what he's got me. I love presents as much as I love surprises, and Grayson indulges me shamelessly. I make it three steps into the room before I realize I'm not alone.

Derek leans against the kitchen island. He's down to his bottom layer, a skin-tight layer of pants and a shirt that leave absolutely nothing to the imagination. His lower half is as thick as his torso. Thick thighs. Thick calves. An ass just as biteable as Grayson's, but in a different way. And his cock... Yeah, it's pressing against that thin layer and letting me know he's thick there, too.

I jerk my gaze back to his face, suddenly remembering that my short silk robe leaves nothing to the imagination, either.

We stare at each other for a long moment. I don't know what to do. Do I pretend everything is normal? Do I ask him if he's okay with this? Do I—

He moves before I can decide on a path forward, pushing off the island and crossing to me. "Grayson said the damnedest thing to me today."

I start to cross my arms over my chest, but it just reminds me that I'm naked under the silk. "Oh?"

"He said he wants to give me a special present for Christmas this year." Derek stops close enough to touch. "A very, very special present this year." His hazel eyes take me in. "You on board with that?"

"Yes," I whisper.

He catches the tie of my robe with a single finger. We both watch as he tugs it loose and lets it drop. "I won't touch you, Emma. Not until it's official." He doesn't move, doesn't seem to breathe. "But give a man something to look forward to."

I shouldn't. I really, really, *really* shouldn't.

But then my hands are moving of their own accord and I'm running my fingers along the edge of my robe, letting it fall open. Derek sinks to his knees, his face right at pussy level, and inhales. "Fuck. He had his mouth all over you just now, didn't he? Came in that room and showed your pussy how much he missed her today?"

My legs are shaking nearly as badly as they did when I came against Grayson's mouth. "Yes."

"Thought so." He's so close, I can feel his exhales against

my damp flesh. Distantly, I can hear the shower still going. I should stop this, would *never* have done something as wanton as stand naked in front of Derek if Grayson wasn't intent on us doing a whole lot more than looking later.

"Have you been good this year, Derek?"

He looks up at me, mirth lingering in his eyes. "Not even a little bit." Then his hands are on my hips and he's nuzzling my pussy. His tongue flicks out and strokes my clit. "I'm bad, Emma. You know that."

I grab his hair, but I don't pull him away like I should. I just hold him still. "You should stop. It's not time yet."

His grin has my heart flipping in my chest. "Don't you want your present?"

This is my present?

I don't stop to think. Don't ask any more questions. Because that's my secret. I want to be bad, too. "Yes, give it to me."

"I'll give it to you, baby." He backs me up to the couch and topples me on it, spreading my thighs wide. And then Derek's mouth is on me for real. He holds me down and explores my pussy with his tongue as if we both aren't listening to the sound of my husband in the shower a single room away. Even though it's dark outside, the light of the kitchen and the lights on the tree chase away any thought of pretending I don't know exactly who is between my legs.

As if he can hear my thoughts, Derek holds my gaze as he stiffens his tongue and slides it inside me. I dig my fingers into his hair and spread my thighs wider. "Suck on my clit."

He moves up to where I urge him, but he's not going fast like I want. He's playing with me. "You taste good, baby."

I don't stop to think about how weird it is that both he and Grayson have called me baby while they've had their tongues all over me. I'm too needy to question this. "You feel good."

"Yeah."

I'm gasping, writhing, trying to make him do exactly what it will take to get me over the edge. "Don't stop."

Derek moves, griping my thighs and shoving them wider yet. He keeps looking at me as he sucks and licks down my pussy and back up again. As if he's trying to gather up every bit of my taste. "Fuck me with your tongue again, Derek. Please."

He does it, covering my pussy with his mouth as he shoves his tongue deep.

And that's when I look up and find my husband leaning against the doorframe. Watching his best friend eat my pussy. I frantically try to yank Derek off me, but he's not going anywhere, and I'm going to hell because I fucking *love* that he refuses to stop. "Grayson," I gasp.

He walks toward the couch, his gaze glued to where Derek is inching me toward an orgasm despite my best efforts. As I watch, Grayson leans down and picks up a white package with red ribbon. My eyes go wide. "Oh *no*." I look down at Derek in horror and the bastard has the audacity to wink at me.

Grayson stalks to the couch and sinks down next to me. Derek gives him a long look and then flicks my clit with his tongue. "You know I always like to take a peek at my presents before Christmas."

"Mmm." Grayson shifts my hair off my shoulder and presses a kiss to my neck. "Does his mouth feel good, Emma?"

My body can't tell if I'm in trouble or being rewarded. "You—you're not mad?"

"No, baby, I'm not mad." Grayson cups my face and presses a devastating kiss my mouth. He nips my bottom lip as he retreats and his next words aren't for me. "Make her come before you go take your shower. *Then* you can enjoy your present properly."

Derek's chuckle reverberates through me. "If you insist." And then he stops fucking around. He holds me down and circles my clit as my husband sits next to me and watches. It's that as much as Derek's expert mouth that has me panting, on the edge of orgasm. "Please. Oh god, don't stop."

Grayson shifts closer and kisses my neck as he palms one breast. Having *both* of their mouths on me... I cry out as I come, as I keep coming, orgasm rolling over me in wave after wave, spurred on my Derek's tongue.

Grayson gives Derek's forehead a nudge. "Go get showered, troublemaker."

"Not sorry." He grins at us and pushes to his feet. I get a close up of a truly impressive cock creating an outline against his tight thermal pants and then he's walking away.

Leaving me to deal with the mess we made of things.

I swallow hard and start to pull my robe back around myself. "I'm sorry. Fuck, I'm sorry."

"Emma." Grayson catches my face and waits for me to calm down enough to actually look at him to continue. "You have nothing to apologize for."

"You sent me out here to get a present, and it took all of fifteen seconds before I was naked and riding Derek's face. I thought that *was* the present, but it wasn't, which means I cheated on y—"

"*No.*" Grayson shakes his head adamantly. "No, fuck that. You were not cheating. I gave you permission. I gave both of you permission. And in case you weren't paying attention, I was only too happy to join in."

I open my mouth to argue, but I can't seem to find my words. "But, that's not what it feels like."

Grayson presses a quick kiss to my lips. "And wasn't it hotter thinking you shouldn't?"

My face flames, answer enough. "If you're not okay with this—"

"Emma." His blue eyes search my face. "Are *you* okay with this?"

Now's the time to put a stop to it, but I'm selfish enough not to want to. I want to keep my relationship with Grayson preserved and indulge myself with Derek. I want to have my cake and eat it, too. I lick my lips. "I'm afraid at how much I want this."

He smiles. My saint of a husband smiles. "Baby, I'll always give you whatever you need, no matter how unconventional. Sounds to me like you need Derek's cock." He stands and tugs me to my feet. "It's time for your *other* present."

I laugh a little. "You are heavily invested in me fucking someone else."

"Yes. But not just anyone else. I'm invested in you fucking Derek in particular." He pulls me along behind him and scoops up the present as we pass it. It's only when we're back in our room that he sets it on the bed. "Now. Open it."

I obey, pulling the red ribbon from the box and carefully lifting the lid. I part the white tissue paper to find a lingerie set the same red as the ribbon. It's intricate and gives the impression of being bondage made of ribbons. I stroke my finger against one band. "This is beautiful."

"He'll have a lot of fun unwrapping you." Grayson tugs on my robe, easing it off my shoulders. "I'm going to have a lot of fun watching."

I take a breath and put away the guilt lingering from letting things with Derek get out of control. If Grayson isn't bothered by it, then I'm being silly for continuing to whip myself over it.

Without the guilt, pure lust rolls over me, rivaled only by my anticipation for things to come. Thirty-six hours of hedonistic indulgence and fucking.

This Christmas is going to be one for the record books.

CHAPTER 4

I look stunning in the lingerie. Truly like the present Grayson's turned me into. While I kneel next to the Christmas tree, he putters around the living room, dimming the lights and building the fire back up. He's wearing lounge pants and nothing else, and I lick my lips at how good he looks. He's not actively training for a marathon right now—he'll start another circuit after the holidays—but he's in some of the best shape of his life. His muscles aren't carved in stone or any of that nonsense but I know firsthand how much lean strength he has coiled in that body. More than enough to haul me around for some sexy manhandling.

I press my thighs together. "Come here."

Grayson gives a dry laugh. "Not with that look on your face. I'll smudge your lipstick."

Lipstick a perfect red to match my lingerie. "Good. It's not going to last the night." Long-stay lip color has nothing on the things I hope we're going to get up to.

"I'll wait my turn."

My body goes tight at the reminder of the game we're playing. His *turn*.

Footsteps draw my attention to the hallway leading to the second bedroom. Derek is wearing lounge pants, too, nearly an identical pair to Grayson's. He drags his hand through his hair and looks at us, all feigned innocence. "What's this?"

Grayson's lips curve into a slow smile. "We've been friends a long time. I thought we'd celebrate Christmas a little differently this year."

Derek's gaze tracks to me and the hunger in his eyes has me fighting not to squirm. It doesn't seem to matter that he had his mouth all over my pussy an hour ago. He looks at me like he isn't sure he can control himself. And then the power of his gaze is gone, turning to Grayson. "If I didn't know better, I'd think you'd wrapped up your wife as a present for me. She's under the Christmas tree and everything."

Grayson strides to me and digs his hand into my hair, tilting my head back a little and arching my back. "I've seen the way you watch her."

"She's beautiful." He shrugs as if that's excuse enough. "And funny and smart and dirty as fuck. I'd have to be dead not to want her."

"Merry Christmas."

If Derek had questions, they were asked on the ski slope, because he stalks toward us, expression intent. "That's one hell of a gift, Grayson."

"You can thank me later."

Derek's gaze doesn't lose its heat as he looks at my husband. "Oh, I will."

Grayson guides me to my feet, catching me under my elbows when my knees nearly buckle with anticipation. I'm standing between these two men, closer than we've ever been before. Soon we're going to *be* closer than we've ever been.

Grayson presses a kiss to the back of my neck and releases me. "Have fun." And then he retreats, walking to the chair next to the fire and sinking into it. It gives him a full view of the room. Of us.

I don't know what I expect, but Derek just studies me, his gaze tracing over me so slowly I think I might die from it. It doesn't seem to matter that he saw me naked earlier. He's looking at me like this is the first time.

He reaches out and slowly runs his fingers through my hair. He's not touching me anywhere *real* but I still feel the contact through my entire body. My breath escapes in a shudder and I have to fight not to lean into him.

I won't touch him first. My pride refuses to allow it. Besides, I'm a gift and a gift doesn't unwrap itself.

His hand drifts down to my shoulder. A relatively innocent thing, somewhere he's touched me before, but the intention is so different. Derek presses his hand to my upper chest, his fingers brushing my collarbones. "I like how you've wrapped my gift, Grayson."

I glance at my husband, watching us with so much heat in his gaze, I'm surprised the room hasn't been engulfed in flames. He leans back in the chair, all studied relaxation. "I thought you might."

Derek drags his fingers lightly down the straps that crisscross my chest, pausing between my breasts, which are barely covered in lace that showcases my nipples. He keeps going, tracing the straps creating a pattern down my stomach and over my hips, to the panties that tease at more than a glimpse of my pussy. The whole thing is complicated and took Grayson's help to get into.

And it looks amazing.

He moves, circling to stand behind me. No doubt studying the way my ass is on display and bared completely of straps. I jump when he brushes me there. He chuckles. "Nervous?"

"No." I'm a liar, but it's the least of my sins right now.

Just like that, Derek stops the tentative teasing. He grabs my hips and pulls me back against his body, pressing himself to me tightly. I gasp at the feeling of his cock against my lower back, but I don't have a chance to figure out what he's doing before he bands one arm around my waist and turns us.

To face Grayson.

Oh god.

Derek backs up, taking me with him, to sit on the couch across from Grayson's chair. He arranges me in his lap, guiding my legs to the outside of his and spreading us both. Putting me on display.

He slides his hands up my sides and then takes my wrists and moves my hands to either side of his hips. Baring me further. I'm not exactly helpless, not being held down, but the feeling is there all the same. Like I'm a toy for him to play with, a doll here only for his amusement and pleasure.

At the thought, desire lights me up like the lights on the Christmas tree.

"Do you know how jealous I was at your wedding?" Derek's voice sounds perfectly normal despite the massive dick pressing against my ass, proving that he's just as affected as I am. He brackets my hips with his big hands and coasts them up to brush his thumbs along the underside of my breasts. "Not the ceremony. Not even all the random shit at the reception." He keeps up that steady motion, idly touching me in a way that was forbidden just a single day ago. "It was when I saw you fucking in the bridal suite."

Grayson snorts. "Peeping in windows, were you?"

"I went for a cigarette. Not my fault you left the windows open and decided to fuck your bride right there where anyone could see you." He moves his hands up slightly, stroking along the scalloped top of the lace bra cups, finally dipping in to drag the fragile fabric down and bare my nipples. "I stood there and watched and knew I'd never be allowed to touch."

I know his words aren't for *me*. Not really. They're for Grayson. I'm just the method of communication.

It doesn't change the fact that I'm nearly panting with desire as he circles my nipples until they pebble to hard points. It doesn't change the fact that my husband watching this only makes it a thousand times hotter.

Derek pinches my nipples and I jerk back against him, fighting down a moan. "Now it's your turn to watch."

Grayson raises his brows. His cock is creating a tent in the front of his lounge pants, but my husband manages to lock down the lust on his face, if only barely. "Tit for tat, is it?"

"Think she'll scream my name when she comes or yours?" He cups my breasts fully now, his palms rasping against my increasingly sensitive nipples.

I bite my lip to keep from begging for more, but I can't stop myself from rolling my hips a little, grinding against his erection. Derek releases one breast and lets his hand drop to cup my pussy. He hisses out a breath against my neck. "She's so wet I can feel her through the lace."

I draw in a shaking breath. "If you don't start unwrapping this present, she's going to unwrap herself."

Derek laughs against my neck. "Impatient."

"Only a little." No point in denying it. Not when we're poised on the brink of something. We've had seven years of teasing. Seven years of denial. Up until this point, I didn't consider it a great trial to ignore my attraction to Derek. I didn't magically become immune to desire just because I'm married, but that doesn't mean I ever would have acted on it. Not with him. Not with anyone.

"All good things are worth the wait, isn't that right, Grayson?"

I love that he keeps bringing my husband into this. I hate it, too. Tonight really isn't about me. Oh, Derek wants me, but that's not enough for him to be going through this slow tease.

That's all about Grayson.

My husband shifts on his chair. "Yes."

Right then and there, I make the decision to drag Grayson into this with us. Not yet. We have to work him into a frenzy before he'll forget himself, forget the rules he's built up in his head to make this work. No one has self-control better than my husband.

No one knows how to break it better than me.

Except maybe Derek.

I settle back against him, still rolling my hips a little. "Just a little touch, Derek."

He ghosts the tips of his fingers up the center of my pussy. I've long since soaked the lace, and it feels good but I'm desperate for actual contact. So desperate, I toss out words designed to prod him into action. "Do you think it only works when we're not supposed to?"

"Baby, we're *not* supposed to." He reaches the top of my panties and dips his fingers in. "You're married to that man over there. To have and to hold, one and only." Slowly, oh so slowly, his fingers descend until he's cupping my pussy, his entire hand wedged into my panties. "And yet it's my hand in your panties right now." His palm drags against my clit as he pushes two fingers into me. "My fingers fucking you right now."

I look at Grayson. I can't help it. I'm sure that Derek's words will sting, but it's not regret on my husband's face. It's pure lust as he watches his best friend's hand move in my panties.

Derek presses an open-mouth kiss to my neck, keeping his pace agonizingly slow. "This pussy is just for him, but I'm playing with it right now. Can't call that anything but wrong, can't you?"

"No," I whisper, spreading my legs wider.

"You get off on that as much as I do." He laughs hoarsely. "Someone says we shouldn't and it's like waving a red flag in front of a bull."

Pleasure builds in slow waves, each spiking a little hotter inside me. "I don't want to want you."

"But that doesn't stop you from clenching around my fingers, does it?" He wedges a third inside me and I can't quite stifle my moan. "It didn't stop you from demanding I fuck you with my tongue earlier."

"That's not fair." I'm bracing myself on the couch on either side of him now, trying to lift my hips to ride his fingers, to drive him deeper.

Derek bands his free arm around my waist and pins me down. "So fucking shameless. You'd ride my hand to orgasm right in front of him, wouldn't you?"

His words feed something dark and hungry inside me. This is just a game. We have permission. But he's right; it doesn't make this feel any less wrong. *Deliciously* wrong.

"Maybe we should stop." But as I say it, I take my hands off the couch and stroke them over his arm. I'm *touching* Derek. "In…just a minute."

He withdraws his fingers. I have half a second to make a protesting noise and then Derek topples me onto the couch. The couch is wide enough for him to lie partially at my side and he wedges himself between me and the back of it.

Just like that, we're kissably close, and this feels a whole lot more intimate than just sitting on his lap. His gaze drops to my lips. I half expect him to ask permission, but we've blown past that several times today already.

Derek kisses me like he has every right to. No hesitation. No reluctance. He takes my mouth like it was his all along, cupping my jaw to angle my head exactly where he wants it so he can plunge deep. He tastes like whiskey, and I'm suddenly afraid that I'm going to get drunk off him.

I shouldn't be too eager. *I* should display some reluctance. But then, I've never been that skilled at being good, not when I can be bad.

I kiss him back with all the pent-up longing I haven't allowed myself to feel. He's nothing like Grayson. My husband is controlled in everything he does, even being wild. His kisses reflect that. Derek's is consuming in a way I don't know if I'll survive. Like he's snapped his leash and he's not going to stop until he's exhausted, which will take a hell of a long time.

I can't wait.

CHAPTER 5

*D*erek finally leans back, and we're both panting as we stare at each other. His eyes contain something that's almost like amazement. "The things I'm going to do to you, Emma."

"Do them," I whisper.

"I don't know if thirty-six hours is enough." He shakes his head, looking dazed. "It'll have to be." As if the deadline spurs him on, he kisses me again and snakes his hand down my stomach to slide into my panties again. This time, he's not teasing. He tries a few different motions out of stroking my clit before he finds the one I like, a soft back and forth that will get me to the edge in no time. He keeps kissing me all the while, drawing my pleasure tighter and tighter, until I'm moaning and would be begging if his tongue wasn't in my mouth.

Derek shifts down to kiss my jaw, using his touch to turn my face to the side. "Look at him, baby." He murmurs. "You're about to come on *my* fingers. Not his."

I meet Grayson's gaze as my orgasm takes me, catching a glimpse of something almost tormented before the pleasure becomes too great and I have to close my eyes. Derek draws it out, sending wave after wave coursing through my body until I feel positively boneless.

He moves, shifting back to kneel between my legs, and running his hands lightly over my body, following the path of the lingerie. "As much as I appreciate the wrapping, how the fuck do I get this off?"

Grayson answers before I can, his voice gone low and hungry. "It's stretchy. Start at the top."

Derek takes him at his word. He carefully fists the straps holding everything in place and tugs it down over my shoulders. The lingerie clings, and I half expect him to jerk it, but he moves methodically, easing it over my body inch by inch, freeing my breasts and then tugging it down my stomach and over my hips. A few seconds later, he's got my legs free and I'm completely naked.

Somehow this feels a thousand times dirtier than wearing the extravagant lingerie. No one but Grayson has seen me like this, without a single bit of clothing and flushed from orgasm, in nearly a decade.

Derek smooths his hands up my legs. "Oh yeah, I like the present a lot, Grayson." He reaches the tops of my thighs and parts my pussy with his thumbs. "So pretty and pink and wet just for me." He licks his lips.

"I want your mouth." I hardly sound like myself.

"One last order of business." He doesn't stop touching me, doesn't stop exploring me with his thumbs as if he didn't have his fingers inside me a few short minutes ago. "Grayson said you're on birth control."

I blink. I don't know why, out of everything, it surprises me that my husband talked about my birth control with the man he wanted me to fuck. "Um, yes."

"I've been tested recently." His expression is painfully

serious. "But if you're not comfortable with me going bare, I won't."

H

"She's comfortable with it," Grayson says.

eat flushes through my body at the idea of Derek's cock inside me without a condom. "It's reckless." I reach down and hook the top of his lounge pants. "I'd have to be so reckless to let you fill me up."

"That's Emma's way of saying she's comfortable with it," Grayson says drily.

DEREK'S EYES darken as he watches me work his pants down his hips, making no move to help or hinder me. "Do you like the idea of going back to him while you're all filled up with my come, baby?"

I have to pause because I can't catch my breath. It's like he's tapping into my filthiest fantasies. "Sounds like you're trying to make this pussy *yours*."

Derek's grin has my heart skipping a few beats. "For the next thirty-six hours, that's exactly what it is. *My* pussy." He braces one hand next to me and runs his other possessively over my body. Pussy, stomach, ribs, breasts, finally settling against my throat for the barest moment. "My Emma."

I give his pants another shove, and he finally decides to help me, both of us engaging in a quick awkward shuffle that results in him naked. And holy shit. I prop myself up on my elbows so I can take him in, and Derek stays kneeling to let me look my fill.

He's breathtaking. I've seen him plenty of times without his shirt, but seeing his thick torso leads into a thick cock framed by thick thighs… Perfection. He's fucking *perfect*.

Grayson's gifted in the cock area, too, but they're shaped different. Derek's dick has a curve that makes my whole body go tight. Or maybe I'm just going out of my mind at the idea of another cock inside me. At *Derek's* cock inside me.

I reach up, distantly noting that my hand is shaking, and run it down his broad chest and rounded stomach. A simple touch, but one I've never allowed myself. Touching leads to other things, and that was always a place I'd never allow myself to go. Now it's a nonissue; at least until the morning after Christmas.

I finally reach his cock and wrap my fist around him. Derek hisses out a breath, and I love that he's enjoying my hands on him as much as I am. I give his cock a tug, towing him gently down toward me. He lowers slowly, letting me lead.

Wicked. This is so incredibly wicked. I drag his cock through my folds and up over my clit. "This is your pussy?"

He's staring intently at what I'm doing, his body one long line of tension. "It's about to be."

I dip his cock inside me, just the tiniest bit, and then guide him back up to my clit. I'm toying with him, trying to snap his leash. From the slight shake as he holds himself back, I'm close to my goal. I circle my clit with the head of his cock. "Grayson fucks me so deep, Derek. So deep and so good. You think you can fuck me better?" Oh god, what am I saying? I don't know, but I can't stop. "You think you can make me come all over this massive cock of yours?"

"Baby, I'm willing to bet on it." He knocks my hand away and fists his cock, resuming the motions I started, dragging himself over me. But he's moving faster, the touch harsher. He notches his cock at my entrance. "It's not really about how good he fucks, is it, Emma? You're insatiable. You want to be bad, and it's *my* cock that gives you that. The one you shouldn't want, the one you're practically panting for." He pushes into me slowly, stopping with just his head inside me. "So, yeah, this pussy is mine. At least for now."

He doesn't give me a chance to respond. He just starts fucking me, wedging his big cock into me a few inches at a time, until he's finally sheathed to the hilt. "How's that cock feel?"

"So good," I pant. "Jesus, you're fucking huge."

He gives me a wide grin. "And you take every inch, don't you, baby?" Derek slides out of me slowly and then slams back in, jolting me up the couch. "That's right. Greedy little pussy, I can feel you clenching around me like you don't want to let me go."

I can't believe this is happening. That I'm on the couch in this vacation rental, getting speared by Derek's massive cock. It feels like a fever dream, like surely this isn't real, no matter how good it feels. "I don't. Don't stop."

"Mmm." He abruptly pulls out of me and pushes me onto my side, settling down behind me. Then he's guiding his cock into me again, using one hand beneath my thigh to spread me up and hold me open for him. "Open your eyes."

I didn't even realize I had them closed. I obey and freeze. I'd almost forgotten Grayson is in the room with us. Shame coats me, but somehow only makes my need all-encompassing.

Then I register exactly what I'm seeing.

Grayson has his cock out. He's stroking himself slowly, as if he wants to make this last, and his gaze coasts over us, jumping from Derek's face to mine, to my breasts, to my pussy...and Derek's cock. His jaw clenches and Grayson gives himself another rough stroke.

Derek moves slowly, an agonizing withdrawal followed by a devastating penetration. "Do you like watching my cock sink into your wife's pussy, Grayson?" His voice hardly sounds like his own. "You get off on watching me spread her wide and force her to take it?"

"I'd think that's obvious." His voice has gone low with desire, but he still manages to sound drily amused.

"Can you really see it from way over there?" Derek hitches my thigh higher. "Don't you want a better look at how I'm enjoying your present?"

Grayson laughs hoarsely. "If you want to make that pussy yours, you have a whole lot of work to do."

My face flames at that. Of course he heard. He's a bare six feet away. Even if we're whispering, there isn't any other sound to detract from it. He'll hear everything.

I just didn't expect him to get off on it as hard as I am.

Derek shifts, sliding his free hand between me and the couch and hooking it around to stroke my clit. "Show your husband how prettily you come on my cock, Emma." He sounds almost angry. "Then I'm going to eat that pussy until you scream *my* name."

For all his anger, he keeps fucking me slowly. Derek alternates stroking my clit with spreading my pussy lips as if wanting me wider yet. Even as wet as I am, it's taken more than few strokes to get to the point where he can slide into me easily. Through it all, he keeps murmuring filth in my ear.

"That's right, baby. You like the feeling of my big cock inside you. So fucking deep." His breath hitches. "Can't get enough of this, can you?"

"No." I'm writhing, but he's got me too thoroughly pinned. He's not moving any faster than he wants to, no matter what *I* want. "God, just *fuck* me, Derek. Please."

He lowers his voice until it's barely a whisper, these words just for me. "I've wanted you for seven fucking years, Emma. Seven years of vacations and listening to him make you come in the next room. Seven years of swimsuits just begging to be untied. Seven years of you looking at me a little too long when you get tipsy, inviting me to drag you off somewhere dark and taste that pussy." He keeps grinding into me, his fingers stroking my clit in the way I need. "To do more than taste you. One kiss and we wouldn't be able to stop. I'd be inside you just like I am right now. Fucking you while your husband is in the other room, totally unaware."

His words make this hotter, dirtier. It doesn't matter that they aren't the truth. They're just fantasy; the evidence of *that* is six feet away with his cock in his fist.

But that's how I like my fantasies. The dirtier, the more forbidden and wrong, the better.

I twist a little to catch his mouth in a quick kiss. God, he tastes so good, I can't stand it. It takes no effort to spin out a new fantasy, wicked and taboo. "I want that." I twist back to look at Grayson, at my husband who will give me anything. "I want it to be wrong. Dirty. Like we shouldn't."

Derek goes still behind me, but Grayson knows me well enough to anticipate my needs. He raises his brows. "You want Derek to seduce you as if it's the first time." Grayson gives his cock another stroke. "You want to be bad, baby. To pretend that I didn't give permission."

I search his face, but there's none of the recrimination I probably deserve. "If that's okay."

Grayson laughs. "Emma, if you think I'm not going to jack myself to the sound of you fucking out of sight, you don't know me as well as you think you do." He gives a surprisingly happy grin. "Anything for you, baby." He crooks his fingers at me. "But if you want penance, you can suck my cock right now before you go play with him. Finish me off."

CHAPTER 6

*D*erek tightens his grip on me and, for a moment, I worry—hope—that he'll keep fucking me despite Grayson's command. But he only gives one last hard thrust and pulls out of me. "Go."

I slide off the couch and crawl to my husband. We don't really do much in the way of formal kink, but I can tell he likes it by the way his eyes light up. I stop when I reach him and slide between his thighs. "Did you like watching that?"

"You're asking a question you already know the answer to." He releases his cock as I reach for it. "The real question is do you want me to catch you two while you're playing out the next fantasy?"

I smile up at him, suddenly so happy I can barely breathe past it. "Now who's asking a question they already know the answer to?"

Grayson shakes his head, his lips curving. "Suck my cock, wife."

"Yes, husband," I whisper. I start to dip down, but then I feel Derek behind me.

He kneels at my back, his cock pressing against my ass, and gathers my hair away from my face. "Give him a show."

I look up to find Grayson watching Derek with a look I can't quite put into words. Because I can't, I focus on the pleasurable task in front of me. Mainly, my husband's cock. I suck him down, achingly aware of Derek at my back, his grip on my hair creating a sexy tugging motion with every stroke.

"Can she deep throat you?" Derek's question surprises me enough that I slow.

Grayson gives that dry laugh, just a little strained around the edges from his pleasure. "Show him, Emma."

Grayson's long enough that we had to practice this. It was a fun game, and it's even more fun now that he's able to fuck my mouth without having to worry about my ability to take him as deep as he wants to go. I suck him down, relaxing my throat until my lips seal completely around him. I'm vaguely aware of Derek cursing softly, but I'm too focused on my task now, on making Grayson feel as good as he's made me feel.

I'm too busy enjoying myself to try to make this quick, though it'd be a lost cause unless he's onboard with the plan. My man has stamina for days. He won't come until he's damn well ready to. He'll make me work for it, and I fucking *love* that.

I feel Derek move at my back, shifting back a little, and then his cock is pushing into me. I freeze, my gaze going up to find Grayson watching me. He flicks a look to Derek. "He's inside you right now, isn't he?" I make a noise of assent and Grayson's expression goes white hot. "Fuck her hard, Derek. Don't hold back."

Derek moves my hair to one hand and his other to my hip, urging me back a little and up so I'm essentially on all fours, though my hands are on Grayson's thighs instead of the floor. Then Derek starts fucking me. The first thrust shoves me forward onto Grayson's cock and I almost gag in surprise.

"That won't do," Grayson murmurs. He moves me off him long enough to slide off the chair and onto his knees. And then he's sliding between my lips, fucking my mouth the same way Derek is fucking my pussy.

I give myself over to them. It's impossible for me to do more than take what they give me in this position, and I do it gladly. Derek's one hand holds my hip in an almost bruising grip, but his other—Grayson slides his hands around my head, and I'm nearly certain that he laces his fingers with Derek's in my hair.

Holy shit.

And then he's coming, driving into my mouth in rough strokes, until I have no choice but to swallow him down. As if I had plans to do anything else. Derek pulls out of me at the last moment and comes on my ass in great spurts. I press my forehead to Grayson's stomach, breathing hard, waiting for my heart to stop trying to race its way out of my chest.

They still haven't let go of each other's hand.

I have half a thought to wonder what they're silently conveying to each other over my back. To wonder if this night is going to take a turn. Grayson seems to decide for all of us, disentangling himself and rising slowly to his feet. He leans down and takes my hand, giving me the support I need to stand. "Get dressed. If you're going to play out the fantasy, do it right."

For a second, I think he's talking to me, but Derek makes a noise that could mean anything and stalks away, grabbing his pants and heading for his bedroom.

Grayson leads me to ours. I barely make it through the door before he's closing it and yanking me into his arms. "That was so fucking hot." He kisses me with something akin to desperation. "Fuck, I can't believe how hot that was." Grayson walks me backward and topples me onto our bed.

"I have come on me!"

"Good." He pins me in place with a hand on my stomach and shoves two fingers into me. "Did his cock feel good inside you, Emma? He stretched you so fucking wide." He pushes a third finger into me. "Too bad he got distracted and didn't make you come."

My whimper becomes a moan as he dips down and licks my clit. "*You* distracted him."

"You get to play out your fantasy, baby." He speaks against my pussy. "But I want to watch you suck his cock later. Fuck, I want to watch it all. It's so fucking hot watching him fuck you."

I don't know what possesses me, but I can't seem to stop spilling truths better left unsaid. "Even when he's saying this pussy is his?"

Grayson arches his brows. "Emma, your pussy is *yours*."

Something like disappointment sinks in my chest. "Oh."

His lips curve. "Ah. Retract that statement." He surges up my body, pinning me in place even as he keeps finger fucking me. "You gave this pussy to me when you said, 'I do.' Riding his cock a few times isn't going to change that." He twists his wrist and strokes my clit with his thumb. "Tell me who this pussy belongs to, Emma."

"You." I'm so close to coming, I'm almost sobbing. "It's your pussy, Grayson."

"That's right." He kisses me hard. "And it pleases me to watch *my* pussy be filled up with Derek's cock. It pleases me to have my wife pretend to be a little slut who's fucking my best friend behind my back." He kisses my neck. "And maybe it will please me to catch you two in the act and punish you." He laughs softly. "Or maybe, if you're quiet, I'll be sleeping too hard to hear the sound of you riding his cock in the living room. Maybe you'll get away with it. No way to tell."

I cling to him as I come so hard my body dissolves into shakes and whimpers. Grayson eases his fingers out of me, presses a kiss to my mouth, and then shifts down to press a thorough kiss to my pussy, as if trying to lick up every bit of orgasm.

Then he sits me up and smiles. "Take a quick shower and put on something that makes it feel real." He kisses me one last time. "I love you."

"I love you, too."

I shower quickly, keeping my hair pinned up so it won't get wet, and after some consideration, put on one of Grayson's knit sweaters and nothing else. I walk out of the bathroom to find that he's changed the bedding and is now reading propped up against the headboard. I hold out my arms. "What do you think?"

"Perfect." He tosses my e-reader onto the foot of the bed. "I'm turning in early, baby. Why don't you go read out in the living room until you get tired enough to join me?"

So we're starting now. Even knowing this is playing out a fantasy, it *feels* so real. How many times over the years have we had a variation of this same conversation? Countless. I often stay up late reading, especially on weekends and vacation. Even vacations where we have Derek accompanying us.

I scoop up the device and come around to give him a quick kiss. "Sleep well, Grayson. I'll be quiet when I come back in."

"Don't worry about it. You know how heavy I sleep." He smiles against my lips. "Take your time."

I half expect to find Derek in the living room already, but it's as empty as it would normally be if this was any other night. I throw another log on the fire and cuddle up on the couch, though it's impossible to focus on my dirty book when I was *just* fucking on this couch. But I try, and when Derek doesn't appear in the next few minutes, I take a deep breath and start to read.

Despite myself, I get caught up in the story. It's just *so good*. Sexy and angsty and full of my kind of reading crack.

"Good book?"

I jump and nearly startle off the couch. "Derek! You surprised me."

He walks into the kitchen and pulls a glass out of the cabinet. "Sorry. I couldn't sleep." He motions to the glass. "Want a drink?"

"Sure." I watch him pour two glasses of whiskey and arch my brows. "That'll make you sleep."

"Maybe." He walks over and sits on the couch next to me. Every other time, he'd have put himself on another chair, or kept a cushion between us. Not this time. He's in the middle, the weight of his body dragging down my cushion and sliding my body toward his. "Here."

I take the glass and sip it while I consider resisting the pull of him. How long am I supposed to hold out? Considering I'm fighting not to climb into his lap, I don't know where the line is.

"How many times have we done this?"

I take another sip of whiskey. "I don't know. A few." He doesn't sleep as soundly as Grayson, so occasionally I'd see him during my late night reading sessions. We've even shared a drink a few times and talked, though never like this. As if we were all too aware that sitting on the same couch and adding alcohol to the mix would be edging into a mistake neither of us wanted to make.

"I'm going to ask you a question, and I'd like you to answer it honestly."

I carefully set the glass on the table and give him my full attention. "Sure."

Derek takes me in slowly, his gaze traveling from my face to my body covered with Grayson's sweater, to my bare legs. "Did you wear that hoping I'd come out here?"

My face heats, but I make myself hold his gaze. As if tonight were the night I'd truly decided to cross that line. "Um." I lick my lips, achingly aware of how he follows the movement. "Maybe." When he doesn't move, doesn't seem to breathe, I continue. "You, uh, you were looking at me today. You're *always* looking at me."

"I want you." He states it as fact, as if he's not crossing a thousand different lines by putting it to voice. "I've wanted you since the first time I saw you, all done up in white and marrying my best friend."

CHAPTER 7

*D*erek's big hand carefully lands on my leg, a few inches above my knee, high enough that there's no mistaking its intention. "I've seen the way you watch me, too."

"You never wear a shirt. You're a handsome man, Derek. Of course I watch you." I shift my legs up to drape them over his lap. Just two friends lounging on a couch, except his hand coasts another inch up my thigh, and my new position has the sweater sliding unforgivably high.

"We shouldn't."

A thrill goes through me. As much as I want to be seduced, there's a certain power in being the one to push us over the edge in this fantasy. I cover Derek's hand with my own, sliding him up another inch. "Did you hear us fucking earlier?"

He tenses. "Impossible not to. You were loud as hell, Emma. Begging him to eat your pussy, to fuck you harder."

"I wanted you to hear." I let my one leg drop back to the floor, and I can tell by the way his jaw clenches that he can see my pussy now.

"That right?"

"Yes."

"And what do you think Grayson will think if I told him that you're out here, flashing your pussy at me in invitation?"

The room feels a thousand degrees hotter than it was a few minutes ago. "He won't say anything at all." I nudge his hand away and move up to straddle him. "Not if you don't tell him." I take his hands and coast them up my thighs to my hips, lifting the sweater as he goes. To my waist, baring my pussy.

"Emma." He's gone hoarse. "You're out here with no panties on. It's enough to make a man like me think you want to fuck him."

"I've been reading this book. It's so fucking hot, Derek. It's got me all wet and needy." I reach between my thighs and slip two fingers into my pussy. I'm so wet, I can hear it. I withdraw and press them to his lips. "See."

Derek holds my gaze as he sucks me deep, his tongue stroking my skin. He gives me one last suck and releases me, his expression almost tormented. "Baby, we can't. Your husband is my best friend."

"Right." Guilt instantly swarms me. "Right, of course. I'm sorry."

But when I try to move off Derek, he keeps me trapped with his hands on my hips. He licks his lips. "It'd be a shame to leave that pussy in need, though. I won't touch, I promise. Just make yourself come." His gaze flicks to my face. "Let me watch."

"Okay," I whisper. Before I can think better of it, I pull the sweater over my head and drop it on the floor by his feet. "It gets in the way."

His gaze consumes me. "Can't have that."

"That's what I'm saying." I cup my breasts, lifting and stroking them, pinching my nipples to peaks. How closely he watches only makes me hotter. How far can I take this before he breaks his promise? Only one way to find out. "I need…" I press my fingers to his mouth again. He sucks them deep, and I withdraw and reach down to stroke my clit with them.

"Does that feel good?"

"Yes." I make a whining noise. "But it's not enough." I reach down and push two fingers into me. "My fingers aren't big enough."

"Fuck," he breathes. "Can't have that. Use mine."

I waste no time grabbing his hand and guiding it between my spread thighs. After some consideration, I arrange him right next to where his cock presses against his pants, two fingers at attention. It feels like I'm moving my very own Derek sex doll, and I can't get over how dirty this is. I sink onto his fingers and moan.

"Shh, Emma." His jaw is tense. "Gotta be quiet or Grayson's going to wake up."

He doesn't move. Just holds perfectly still as I slide up and down his fingers and stroke my clit. The fact that I'm naked and completely exposed only makes this hotter. Grayson could walk out at any time and I'd have no way to pretend I'm doing anything other than riding his best friend's fingers.

"Fuck, you're so sexy." He makes a pained sound. "Rub your tits on my face, baby. Use me to make yourself good."

"Like a toy."

"Exactly like that." He nods slowly. "You're not cheating on Grayson when you feed a dildo into that tight little pussy, are you? I'm your toy. Use me."

I lift myself off his fingers and press my breasts together to rub myself against his face. No matter what Derek says about being a toy, that doesn't stop him from licking my nipples and sucking them into his mouth, first one side and then the other. His beard only adds to the sensation. I feel his hands moving against my thighs, but I don't realize his intent until I sink down and his bare cock is there. I reach down and hold him still as I rub myself along his length. "Just another toy?"

"Aren't you empty, baby? Wouldn't it be good to be filled with that toy in your hand?"

Now it's my turn to play the reluctant party. "I don't know." I arch up, offering him my breasts again. "I can't think."

"Then don't think." He's actively touching me now. Grabbing my ass and squeezing, his fingers skating down the lower curve to guide me forward and up. And then down his stomach, until the head of his cock is there. Derek exhales and then he's there at my entrance. "Just a little, baby. Just the tip hardly counts."

"Derek, we shouldn't." But I roll my hips to take him inside. "Oh fuck, that feels good." I do it again, working my way down his length. "Just one stroke. Just one isn't really fucking."

"That's right baby. Only one stroke doesn't count." He pulls me tight against him, sealing us together.

He felt good behind me, but this position feels a thousand times hotter. Or maybe that's the fantasy doing it, playing at cheating on my husband. I rock on his cock, but he doesn't let me put any distance between us. When I whimper, Derek leans back against the couch, reclining until my tits are in his face. "It's still only one stroke as long as I don't leave you." He grinds me down on him, drawing forth another whimper. "And why would I want to leave this hot, tight pussy? You're so wet, Emma. Just for me."

I dig my fingers into his hair and pull his head to my breasts. "I'm so close to coming. This is so wrong. We shouldn't be doing this."

He keeps pulsing up into me, grinding me on his cock, against his stomach. It's so fucking filthy, a complete violation of the rules we just created. "It's only one stroke, Emma. Just one little stroke. It hardly counts." He sucks hard on one nipple, making me whimper. "But, fuck, I could come from this stroke alone."

I'm so close, I'm panting. "You can't, Derek. If you come inside me, he'll know. He'll catch us."

"It's okay, baby." He nips the underside of my breast and soothes it with his tongue. "If I come inside you, I'll lick that pussy clean. I promise. He'll never know that you were out here, riding my cock, taking me so fucking deep, using me like your own personal sex toy."

It's too much. I come hard, writhing on his cock, moaning and whimpering and forgetting entirely that we're supposed to be quiet. Derek keeps me sealed to him, something like wonder flickering across his expression. "Fuck, Emma. You're perfection."

I feel loose and downright punch-drunk. I roll my hips, working myself on his cock as much as he'll allow. "I can't believe we're doing this. We need to stop."

"Too late, Emma. Too fucking late. You've let me inside and I've spent seven long years thinking about how I'd fuck you if given a chance." His hands tighten on my hips. "Do you really want me to stop?" A devastating grin spreads across his mouth. "Or do you want me to fuck you properly?"

There's only ever been one answer to that question, and it's the one I give him now. "Don't stop."

He loops an arm around my waist and turns, laying me down on the couch. I half expect him to cover me with his body, but Derek stays kneeling between my spread legs. He pushes my thighs up and wide and thrusts slowly into me. "I couldn't see properly before."

I prop myself up on my elbows as best I can and watch his cock disappear into me, captivated by the sight. "You feel so good," I gasp.

"Looks just as good." He pulls halfway out and delivers a series of shallow thrusts that have me fighting not to close my eyes. "You like the sight of my cock in your pussy, Emma? Spreading you so fucking wide and you just take it, don't you? You're greedy for it."

"*Yes*." I moan, cupping my breasts and plucking at my nipples. He promised to fuck me properly, but he's teasing and it's driving me crazy. "Hurry. He might wake up."

"Fuck no, I'm not rushing this." He sinks into me to the hilt and then starts his slow retreat. "Look down, Emma. That's not your husband's cock that's wet with your orgasm. It's not Grayson's cock inside you right now, making you feel so good. It's not *his* cock that you're practically begging for."

His words are dirty and a little mean and I eat them up. I flop back onto the couch and run my hands up his arms and over his chest. "You're right. It's not his cock spreading me so wide right now." I skate my fingers down his stomach. "It's yours." I finally, finally, look up into his eyes. He's looking at me like he never wants this to end, like he's as caught up in the whole thing as I am. I lick my lips. "Fuck me hard, Derek. Make me come so hard, I have to muffle my screams or I'll wake him up and he'll come in here and see you fucking me with that giant cock of yours."

He loops his arms under my thighs, holding me open for him even as he leans down and presses his big body against mine. Derek kisses me as he keeps up that slow, thorough fucking. He leaves my mouth and kisses along my jaw and lowers his voice. "Do you remember that trip three years ago?"

Instantly, I know what he's talking about.

Another holiday vacation, another destination. This one was in the Caribbean, a massive suite that Grayson had insisted on because there was no reason for us and Derek to have separate hotel rooms. I draw in a shuddering breath and kiss his shoulder, his neck. "You went to bed early." I moan as he thrusts deep and grinds into me, the angle rubbing against my G-spot. "Grayson and I had a few more drinks."

"You did more than that." Derek's picking up his pace slowly, working that spot inside me with each swivel of his hips. "I came out for some water and there you were on the couch. He had your top shoved up and was worshiping those perfect breasts of yours." He nips my earlobe. "And then he pulled off your skirt and ate that pretty pussy."

I go still. "You were watching that long?" I'd seen him, but not until later, and then only a glimpse. I thought he'd walked in and almost instantly retreated. *That* was hot on its own. But what he's describing? "I didn't see you."

"No shit you didn't see me." He chuckles against my skin and bends down to kiss along the upper curves of my right breast. "You were too busy riding your husband's mouth. Digging your hands into his hair and rubbing your pussy all over his face like the wanton thing you are."

I remember. It'd been *so* dirty to have Grayson going down on me when Derek could walk in on us at any time. I hadn't tried to be quiet. "And then I pushed him down onto the floor and rode his cock." *That* was when I'd looked up and saw Derek standing in the shadows of the hallway, watching us hungrily. I hadn't tried to cover myself, hadn't even thought of stopping. I'd just kept fucking Grayson until I'd come again. By the time we finished, Derek was nowhere to be seen and part of me had decided to pretend that I'd imagined it.

"After seeing that, I couldn't sleep. I kept thinking about how good you looked, how hot it was to watch you." He kisses me again and leverages himself up, his gaze raking down my body. "I went out to the living room again later, half hoping you were doing some of your late night reading."

I inhale sharply. "I wouldn't be able to pretend I didn't know you saw us if you had."

"I know." He cups my breasts together and lavishes them with his mouth. He's still got my legs spread obscenely and it's almost uncomfortable, but I don't care because his cock is impossibly deep in this position and I *love* how his mouth feels on my nipples. "I wouldn't have said a single damn thing."

Another orgasm is bearing down on me, so powerful I can barely speak. "No?"

"No. I would have knelt in the exact same position Grayson did." His voice has gone as hard and rough as his fucking. "Just flipped up that skirt and kissed that pussy hello. And after you came all over my face, I'd be fucking you. Just. Like. This." He bites my breast, just hard enough to hurt, hard enough to make me moan, loud and long. "So deep in that pussy, aren't I, Emma?"

"Yes," I gasp.

"Let me fill you up." He barely sounds like himself. "Let me pump you full of my come, baby. I promise he'll never know." Derek thrusts into me hard. "I like the idea of you going back to him with me dripping down your thighs. A reminder that you might be married to him, but this pussy belongs to *me*."

Grayson's voice sounds from far too close. "I hardly think so."

CHAPTER 8

*W*e both freeze. I look over, my heart in my throat, to find Grayson standing on the other side of the coffee table, watching us. "I can explain." I push at Derek, but he doesn't move, his cock still half inside me.

Grayson arches his brows. "By all means. Don't stop on my account. My best friend is balls deep in my wife while I was in the next room. If you're that fucking shameless, you're shameless enough to keep going."

"Grayson—"

But Derek has a strange look in his eye. Just like before. Almost as if he's angry. "She was feeling needy. I took care of her. Simple as that."

"Simple as that." Grayson narrows his eyes and rounds the coffee table in slow, measured steps. I watch him, my heart beating so fast I feel light-headed. He looks furious, so furious this might be real if not for the hard-on pressing against the front of his pants.

"Yeah, simple as that." Derek lifts himself a little, which sinks his cock deeper into me. "And maybe she was craving *my* cock."

53

"Your cock. Your come." Grayson finally looks at me, his gaze lingering where Derek's cock spears me, moving up over my stomach to where my breasts are reddened from his mouth and beard, finally settling on my face. "You want my best friend's come, wife?" He doesn't wait for me to formulate an answer. "Then you'd best take it."

Grayson moves, quick as a snake, and wraps his hand around Derek's cock, forcing the other man out of me. I gasp and Derek groans, and we both watch Grayson jack him in shock. My husband is as intimidating as I've ever seen him, blue eyes stormy, his jaw clenched. "But that's *my* pussy, and I'm the only one who comes in it. You have to earn that privilege, Derek, and you sure as shit won't do it by fucking my wife behind my back."

Derek is gasping like he's running a marathon, his gaze glued to Grayson's fist around his cock. And then he groans, low and sexy, and he's coming. Grayson points his cock at my pussy, directing his come in spurts across my heated flesh. I flinch at the feeling, but I can't help spreading my thighs even wider, nearly whimpering by how dirty this is.

Grayson shoves Derek back onto the couch and the other man allows himself to sprawl there, shock still written across his features. My husband drives two fingers into me. "You want his come, Emma? You're so desperate for another man, for my best fucking friend, that you're out here like a little slut, taking his cock deep? I'll give you his come." He withdraws and drags his fingers through Derek's come, shoving them deep again. Again and again, until he's driven nearly every bit inside me.

I can't stop shaking. I'm trying to hold still, but I can't help lifting my hips in invitation every time he touches me. "Please."

"Please what?" He palms my pussy, smearing his hand through the stickiness left over. "You go through all that effort to fuck someone else and he doesn't give it to you right?" He looks at Derek and laughs harshly. "Don't worry. I'll show you how it's done."

Grayson and I have played countless games over the years. I have never, ever seen him like this. Almost cruel in the sexiest way possible. He flicks a look at me and raises his brows. "Well, Emma? You need this cock?"

"Yes." I reach for his pants with shaking hands. "Yes, I need your cock. Please. Right now."

"That's right, baby. You don't have to go anywhere else to get what you need, do you?" He stands up and steps out of his pants. I lick my lips at the sight of his cock, as if I didn't have him down my throat earlier tonight. Grayson scoops his arm under my waist and practically drops me on top of Derek. We both freeze, but my husband doesn't hesitate to grab my hips and sink inside me. For all the filthy talk of Derek's massive cock, Grayson is just as big, and he knows how to hit all the right places, exactly what it takes to get me off.

He's fucking me on top of Derek.

Grayson braces one hand on either side of my hips—on either side of Derek's hips—and shoots his best friend a dark look. "If you're going to be here, do something useful. Play with her tits."

I feel Derek's breath shudder out and then he's cupping my breasts in his big hands. Grayson finds the angle I love the most and begins fucking me in short, brutal strokes. Another sharp look at Derek. "One hand on her clit. Short, gentle vertical strokes. Don't deviate."

Holy shit.

Derek hesitates and then reaches down to stroke my clit exactly as Grayson commands, the motion designed to send me to the moon. Within a few minutes of their combined efforts, my toes are curling and I'm fighting to stay still. "I'm sorry. I'm so fucking sorry."

"No, you're not." Grayson's lips curve. "Now come for me, Emma."

Another stroke, a second, and then I'm coming so hard I scream and Grayson has to use his body to hold me down. He keeps pumping slowly, toying with my pleasure. I become aware of several things in waves. Derek's hard cock pressed against my ass. Derek's hands on my body, but also touching Grayson. Their faces very, very close together over my shoulder.

I shift a little to the side and look. Grayson's mouth is so close to Derek's that their rough breathing mingles. They're staring at each other like they've never seen the other before. Like they haven't been giving long looks when they thought the other wasn't paying attention since I've known them... likely longer than that.

"Do it," I whisper.

My husband kisses Derek. The sight of it takes my breath away. They're both so fucking powerful, and they're wrestling with that power with me between them. Tongues and teeth and a kiss that's just shy of vicious.

Grayson starts moving inside me again, continuing to fuck me while he has his tongue down Derek's throat, while his hands are moving behind me on the other man's body. Derek starts thrusting against my ass, reaching up to pull Grayson closer.

My husband is the one to break the kiss. "I want to feel you inside her while I'm fucking her deep."

I open my mouth to suggest they just fuck without me in between, but Derek is already nodding. "Yes. I want that."

Grayson pulls out of me. He lifts me easily, turns me, and pushes me down to straddle Derek. "Fuck him slow, Emma. I'll be right back."

We both listen to his footsteps retreat into the bedroom. I lean back enough to give Derek a long look. "You know—"

"No."

"You don't even know what I'm about to say." They have even more pent-up lust than Derek and I do. Why the hell are they both fighting this so hard?

He fists his cock and holds my hip as he eases into me. I whimper a little. If I survive this thirty-six hours, I'm going to be sore as hell. I don't care. I don't want to stop. I rock a little. "Derek—"

"Emma, I am your friend and I'm going to fuck you until we're both unconscious and then fuck you again until our time's up, so understand that I'm saying this with love." He drags me down his cock. "Mind your own goddamn business."

"Mmm." I can hear Grayson moving around in our room. "And it's not my business that my husband's going to fuck my ass while you fuck my pussy so you can *feel each other* inside me?"

Derek gives me a smirk that's almost convincing. "Baby, you're focusing on the wrong part of what happens next." He bounces me on his cock. "You're already filled up with me. How much more do you think you're going to be filled when his giant cock is in your ass? Do you think you can take it?"

"She had damn well better." Grayson walks back into the living room naked, a bottle of lube in his hand. He gives us a long look. "My little slut of a wife needs more than one cock to keep her happy right now, so that's what she gets."

I shiver on Derek's dick and look over my shoulder at my husband. "I love you."

"And yet no doubt the next time I turn around, Derek's going to have his tongue in your pussy."

"Guilty." Derek laughs.

Grayson snorts. "That's what I thought." He smooths a hand up my back, urging us both down until Derek's slouched against the back of the couch. My breasts press against his chest and we look at each other for a long moment. It seems the most natural thing to kiss him, to tell him without words how much I'm enjoying this, enjoying *him*.

Then my husband spreads lube over my ass and his cock is there. He doesn't give me much time to prepare, just eases the head into me. I break my kiss and gasp. Derek looks at my face and then over my shoulder at Grayson. "Go slower."

"She can take it. Emma loves anal."

It's the truth, but it's a whole different feeling to have him pressing slowly into me when I'm already filled up with another massive cock. I tense before I can help it. "Hold on."

"Relax, baby." Grayson doesn't push any farther inside me but his chest brushes my back as he moves my hair out of the way and starts kissing the back of my neck. Just like that, I relax again and rock back into him. He chuckles against my skin. "That's right. That feels good, doesn't it?"

"Yes." I shift again, and Derek clamps down on my hips, holding me still. I make a sound of protest but then his mouth is on the front of my neck. It feels so freaking good. I melt between them and Grayson works his cock the rest of the way inside me.

He curses long and hard. "Fuck, baby, you're tight as hell with him inside you."

I move my hips as much as I can and moan. "You both feel so big." It's almost too much, but I don't want to stop. I don't *ever* want to stop.

The thought is almost enough to drive back my desire. There's a deadline on this, no matter how good it feels now. A Christmas fling is something entirely different than fucking Derek on the side. The latter is messy as hell, and I value my relationship with Grayson too much to even suggest it.

But that doesn't mean I'm not going to enjoy the hell out

of his cock in the meantime.

"You feel me?"

For a second, I think my husband is talking to me, but Derek answers before I can find the words. "Yeah," he grits out. "I feel you."

Grayson withdraws a little and thrusts, and we all moan. He braces one knee on the couch on the outside of mine and bears down, forcing me closer to Derek, forcing his cock deeper yet. I whimper and then moan, writhing on their cocks as Grayson leans over my shoulder and kisses Derek again. Their hands are everywhere, touching each other, pulling each other closer, which drives them deeper inside me. I am merely the vessel for their lust and, fuck, it's so hot I can barely stand it. I moan and roll my hips as much as I can, chasing the building pressure deep inside me.

Derek and Grayson start fucking me in short thrusts, as if they can't stand the idea of moving far enough from each other that they'd have to stop kissing. I'm so close, but I can't get there. I'm sobbing and trying to move, but they have me too effectively wrapped up. I'm helpless to do anything but take it.

And then Grayson slips his hand between my and Derek's body and strokes my clit. He keeps kissing Derek and touching me and they're so impossibly deep that I completely lose it. I bury my face in Derek's neck and sob as I come harder than I could have thought possible.

They don't stop.

In fact, they slow down, like they want this to last as long as it possibly can, like the second they orgasm, they have to go back to pretending they're only making out because I'm between them. Right then and there, I dazedly decide to make a gift of Derek to my husband.

It's Christmas, after all. There are no rules when it's Christmas.

CHAPTER 9

I can't stop shaking, so over-sensitized that the feeling of them inside me is almost too much. And they just keep fucking. Finally, just when I'm on the verge of begging, Derek moans into Grayson's mouth and fucks up hard into me. I didn't think I could come again. I truly didn't. But the force of his orgasm sets Grayson moving, fucking my ass roughly as Derek pumps into me, and my body spasms, forcing shrieks from my lips. Grayson pulls out at last moment and comes across my ass and back, and then he collapses on the couch next to us. "Fuck."

"Fuck's about right." Derek laughs a little, but it sounds forced as hell. Especially when I catch him stroking Grayson's arm with his knuckles. A touch that might be acci-dental, but I don't think so. That, more than anything, gives me the strength to speak. "I want us all in bed together tonight."

Derek tenses, but I keep going. "Thirty-six hours, Derek. Tell me you don't want the option of waking up with my mouth around your cock. Or even just slipping inside me while we're still mostly asleep." I lean up and kiss him, tasting my husband on his lips. "Please. Please say yes."

He sighs in a way that's almost resigned. "Yes."

It takes a little while to get there. We shower off the mess from our fucking and Derek retreats to his bedroom to grab an extra pillow. The king sized bed is plenty big enough for three, and I'm not even remotely surprised when they put me between them. I expect to take a while to fall asleep, but I drift off almost immediately, cradled between the warmth of Derek and Grayson's bodies.

At one point in the middle of the night, I have to get up to pee, and when I come back, Grayson has moved, rolling nearly to the middle of the bed. I snort and take his spot, falling asleep again almost immediately.

I wake up to the sound almost like moan.

Opening my eyes, I'm not even surprised to find Derek draped over Grayson's chest, his head buried in my husband's throat. Grayson's eyes are open, and I know him well enough to read the question in his eyes. *Can I?*

I nod quickly. Just in case he misses that obvious answer, I mouth, *Do it.* I bite my lip. *Fuck him.*

Grayson searches my face, but seems content with what he finds there. I'm being perfectly honest in what I want right now. No games. No tricks. My husband wants Derek, and I want Grayson to have him.

He finally gives a brief smile and then focuses on the sleeping man on his chest. Grayson feathers his fingers through Derek's hair and strokes the man's arm with his other hand. Derek groans and his hips thrust forward. He opens his eyes, sees me, and goes still.

Grayson doesn't give him a chance to think too hard about anything. He cups his friend's face and kisses him. Derek almost seems like he might resist, but then he moans and his hands are on Grayson's body.

I bite my lip as I watch them. They're making out and thrusting and I can't help but reach over and tug the blankets down so I can see how they're grinding their cocks against each other. It's almost a frenzy, moans and grunts and the sound of skin against skin.

Desire surges and I slip my hand between my thighs to stroke my clit. Will they come from this alone, spurting onto each other's stomachs, mixing their semen like that? God, I hope so.

Grayson digs his fingers into Derek's hair and pulls his head back so he can slip down and kiss his neck. Derek looks at me with glazed eyes. "We're leaving Emma out."

"I'm enjoying the show." I sound nearly as breathy as he does.

I didn't understand before, not truly. I was selfish enough to take the gift Grayson offered without thinking about what he got out of it. Now I get it. They're beautiful together. Sexy as shit. And knowing they're fulfilling a need that's been burning between them for years? It just makes it hotter. I don't feel a flicker of jealousy at the thought of Grayson and Derek having sex. Not even a little bit.

Now Grayson's looking at me, too, something wicked lurking in the curve of his lips. "Come here, baby."

I almost protest so they'll keep going without me, but something about the way Derek seems to be holding his breath has me moving closer. He's the one who grabs me around the hips and lets himself flop off Grayson's chest, hauling me with him so that I'm sprawled across both men.

Using me as a buffer again.

He kisses me before I can call him on it. I tense, but Grayson runs his hands over my body, shifting so that I lay between them. He's kissing my neck even as Derek takes my mouth, their hands tangling up on my body. Because as much as they're enjoying this, they really want to be fucking each other right now.

I pull away and sit up. It takes some maneuvering to turn around to face them, mostly because I keep having to smack their hands away. "Hold on. I can't think when you're touching me."

"Now isn't the time for thinking."

I frown at my husband. He's been spearheading this thing the whole time and then he kissed Derek again this morning, and *now* he's going to put on the brakes and toss me to his best friend like a runner's-up prize? I don't think so.

It's not even about my pride. Grayson has been more than generous in giving me everything I've ever asked for, and more than a few things I haven't had the courage to put into voice until he prodded the truth from me. His attraction to Derek falls into the latter category for him. He can't admit it, and if left to his own devices, he'll keep me between them for the entirety of this last twenty-four hours.

I don't know *why* he's holding back, either. He's had boyfriends in the past before we got together. Derek has as well. Is it because he doesn't want to lose the friendship?

That ship has long since sailed. It left the harbor right around the first time I came all over Derek's face. We've gone too far to go back. There's only forward.

I run my hands up both their chests. "Derek's gift is covered."

Grayson narrows his eyes, already sensing a trap. "Uh huh."

"I want *my* gift."

Derek laughs. "Fucking both of us isn't good enough for you, Emma?"

"Having sex with me is *your* gift." I trail my hands back down their chest to their stomachs. They're so different and both so sexy. I almost pause, but I've never been that good at impulse control. I wrap my hands around each of their cocks and give them a slow stroke. "Please, Grayson. I promise you'll like it."

He gives me an indulgent smile that's only a little tight around the edges. "Anything for you, Emma."

"No matter what it is?" I squeeze his cock, making him clench his jaw. "Promise?"

"No matter what it is," he grits out.

I turn my attention to Derek. "Can you promise me the same?" I grip his cock and rub my thumb over the slit, smearing the drop of moisture I find there. "Please, Derek."

He huffs out a breath, but not like he's happy. "Yeah, Emma. Whatever you want."

Gotcha.

I give both their cocks one last stroke, debating how far to push this. They just need enough of a nudge to get there on their own. I bite my bottom lip. "I want to ride your face while Grayson sucks your cock."

Derek tenses, very carefully not looking at Grayson. "I don't know if that's such a good idea."

Oh, this is ridiculous. I release them and sit back. "Give me one good reason you two shouldn't fuck? It's silly to keep me between you when you obviously want each other, too."

Grayson sighs. "We're friends."

"And?" I wait, but no other answer seems forthcoming. "Are we not friends, Derek?" A little sliver of hurt escapes in my tone. Obviously, Derek and I were never as close as he and Grayson, and there was the sexual tension neither one of us could get rid of, but... I thought we were friends.

"Of course we are."

The coiling thing in my chest relaxes a little. "We've already crossed so many lines together. Things are going to change no matter what. Why not cross a few more?"

Derek finally looks at Grayson, so I do, too. The sheer

longing on my husband's face nearly knocks me on my ass. The only other person I've ever seen him look at like that is me. It just confirms that this is the right decision. He wants Derek. I mean for Grayson to have him.

Derek clears his throat. "If you're sure."

I don't know if he's talking to me or my husband, but Grayson is the one who answers. "I'm sure. Our friendship has gone through some shit. This won't break it."

I find myself holding my breath as they lean in and kiss, a messy tangling of tongues that has them both moaning a little. Derek breaks the kiss with a curse. "Get up here, Emma." He doesn't wait for me to move, just loops me around the waist and lifts me up to straddle his face as if I weigh nothing at all. His breath ghosts against my clit. "Sore?"

"I can take more," I breathe.

"That's our girl." Before I can process the *our* in that statement, his tongue is there, easing over me in a lazy lick.

I lean forward and brace my hands on his wide chest, spreading my legs a bit more to give him better access. As I do, I watch Grayson crawl to kneel between Derek's big thighs. He holds my gaze for a long moment and even knowing him so well, I can't begin to say what his blue eyes contain. He dips down and I watch him take Derek's cock into his mouth, holding my gaze the whole time.

I almost come on the spot.

Derek moans against my pussy and then he's eating me out frantically. It's messy and so fucking good that I whimper. Or maybe I'm whimpering because watching my husband suck Derek's cock is like my own personal porno that I didn't even know I wanted. It is so beyond hot. So beyond anything I'd ever thought to ask for.

I want more.

More for me. More for him.

CHAPTER 10

I fight my own orgasm, fight not to close my eyes and miss a moment of this. It doesn't seem to matter what I want. My body takes over, pleasure washing over me in waves. God, it's so good. Too good. Can a person die from too much pleasure?

I barely manage to open my eyes in time to watch Derek lace his fingers through Grayson's hair and move his hips, beginning to fuck my husband's mouth. I can tell the exact moment he comes because Grayson moans around his cock. *Oh my god.* I move before I have a chance to think, climbing down Derek's body to haul Grayson up and kiss him. I can taste Derek's saltiness on his tongue and it drives me crazy.

Grayson topples me back onto Derek's chest and moves up between our spread legs. He looks down at me and then over my shoulder at Derek. He doesn't have to speak. His thoughts are written all over his face, boiled down to a single possessive word. *Mine.*

He guides his cock into me, just too shy of being too rough. I start to reach for him, but Derek catches my wrists. "You've caused enough trouble today."

"It won't be enough until you fuck."

His laugh is strained. "Jesus, Emma."

"She has no problem asking for what she wants." Grayson begins moving, fucking me against his best friend's chest as Derek holds me down. Each stroke feels like he's claiming me, like he's making a promise to Derek.

Derek shifts my wrists to one of his big hands and skates the other down my stomach to play with my clit as Grayson fucks me.

I'll never get used to this. The sheer *decadence* of having two sets of hands on me. Of being pressed between two bodies. It's a fast-growing addiction I don't have the self-preservation to curtail. I want, want, want. More, more, more. I come again, and Grayson follows me over the edge, grinding into me, his eyes gone wild. He half-slumps onto us and laughs roughly. "I'm going to crush you."

"I can take it," Derek growls at my back.

"Still." Grayson shifts to the side and takes me with him, dragging us all over onto our sides. He props his head in his hand and gives a startling open grin. "Merry Christmas."

It is Christmas, isn't it?

I stretch between them, enjoying the feeling of my skin rubbing against theirs on either side. "Merry Christmas."

Derek's stomach chooses that moment to make a large growling sound. Grayson laughs a little. "I'll get breakfast started." When I start to rise, he gives my shoulder a nudge. "Stay. I'll call when it's ready."

I watch him rise and stride out of the room. If I didn't know better, I'd say my husband is running from what he just did. It doesn't make any sense. The line's been crossed. Last night. This morning. There's no point in trying to go back. Why would he want to?

Derek's arms come around me and he pulls me back

against his chest. "Pretty sure this goes down as most memorable Christmas ever."

"Pretty sure?" I inject my tone with some mock outrage and turn in his arms. "You're going to irreparably damage my self-esteem if you tell me I don't measure up to the bicycle you got when you were eight."

He grins. "It was a really cool bike. It had flames on it and everything."

"So rude." I laugh and snuggle closer. "Merry Christmas, Derek."

His expression goes soft and he smooths my hair back from my face. "Merry Christmas, Emma."

It strikes me that this is the final day. Christmas. By morning tomorrow, we'll go back to being the two most important people in Grayson's life who *don't* exchange bodily fluids. Something like panic flutters in my chest. I thought it would be simple to put Derek back in the "safe" box in my mind once this was over, but now I don't know if it's possible. "What if this was a mistake?"

His fingers feather over my temple. "This stops when you want it to. If you're not comfortable with it, we can stop now."

But what if I don't want it to stop?

I don't say it. It feels like a betrayal to take this gift Grayson gave me—gave us—to ask for more. "I'm okay." I manage a smile. "It's just a little surreal that this is happening at all."

"Fuck yeah." He leans down and brushes his mouth against mine.

I should leave it at that, but I've never been good at sitting back and letting something I want drift past. I run my hands up his broad chest. "It's the same for you, you know. If you want to stop, we stop." I hesitate. "If you don't want to fuck Grayson, you don't have to. I just—"

Derek catches my mouth with his. He kisses me hard, hard enough that I can't help writhing a little, my body already demanding more despite the two outstanding orgasms I experienced not too long ago. When he finally lifts his head, we're both breathing hard. He runs a big hand down my back and over my ass. "It's complicated."

"That's not an answer."

"Guess not." His gaze falls to my mouth and he looks like he's considering kissing me until I forget what we were talking about. "But it's the truth. It's complicated."

"Uncomplicate it."

Derek huffs out a laugh, though it sounds strained. "Grayson is…" He rolls onto his back, but keeps me tucked against his side. "We've been friends for most of our lives."

I have to press my lips together to keep from peppering him with questions, from dragging his thoughts out one by one. He'll tell me or he won't. I have to learn some freaking patience.

While I'm wrestling with myself, he keeps going. "There was always something more, but the timing was never right, you know? We went to separate colleges and I had a boyfriend when I came back home for Christmas. Then I was single at graduation, but he was talking about moving in with that guy he's been fucking semi-regularly." He studies the ceiling as if it's the most interesting thing in the world. "We were both single for a hot minute before he met you, but I was stuck in London for a few months working with a new client. By the time I got back, he'd met you and that was that."

My chest pangs and I sit up. "I didn't know."

"We've never talked about it." He still isn't looking at me. "Easier to just be friends and stay in each other's lives. And, fuck, Emma, I *like* you. You're cool as shit, and you're good for him. He lights up whenever you walk into a room. I can't

69

hold it against either of you." Derek gives a faint smile. "Though I'm not even going to lie; wanting both of you has been irritating as fuck."

"Derek—"

"It's enough. It *will* be enough." He moves before I can come up with a response, toppling me back to the bed and kissing me hard. He slides down my body, pausing to worship my breasts for several long moments before he kisses his way down my stomach.

"Derek, we haven't—" My breath hisses out at the first long drag of his tongue. "You can't distract me with this."

"Mmm." He works my clit slowly. "If you say so."

"If you don't want to—"

He exhales harshly and lifts his head. "I want to, Emma. I want to so fucking bad, I can barely stand it. My control is hanging by a thread. So yeah, if it happens today, I'll happily fuck Grayson. Is that what you want to hear?"

"Yes."

He laughs, and this time it doesn't sound quite so rough. "But not yet. First I'm going to give your pretty pussy the attention it deserves."

I lace my fingers through his hair and lift my hips. "I still can't believe we're doing this." There are other things that need to be said, subjects that need to be broached, but now isn't the time. I've pushed both Derek and Grayson enough for the moment. Even I know when to dial it back. Sometimes. "It feels wicked."

"You *taste* wicked." He gives me another lick. "Even more wicked than normal because I can taste *him* in you."

I rub myself against his mouth a little. "You did promise to clean me up."

Derek's laugh vibrates through my body. "That I did." He takes his time, eating me out slowly as if he doesn't really give a fuck if I come or not. As if he's doing it purely for the pleasure of having my taste on his tongue. Or maybe it's the taste of Grayson that has him kissing my pussy so thoroughly.

Time ceases to have meaning. There is just this moment, this pleasure. At some point, I look up and find Grayson leaning against the doorframe and watching us. The heat in his eyes… God, he looks at us like he owns us. So possessive. So sexy.

He clears his throat. "Breakfast is ready."

Derek sucks on my clit. "I'm not done." His big hands bracket my thighs, holding me in place. The reality of have him licking my pussy while my husband watches has my orgasm drawing closer.

And then it gets better because Grayson crosses to the bed and leans down to grip the back of Derek's thick neck. "You can have her for brunch, too, if you want, but you both need an actual meal. Make Emma come. Now." When Derek just keeps up those long, lazy licks, Grayson curses. "Fine. I'll do it myself." He reaches down with his free hand and spears me with two fingers. It takes him half a second to find my G-spot and then I'm orgasming. My toes curl and my spine arches and I think I might be shrieking but I can't hear myself over the buzzing in my head.

Grayson tows Derek up and kisses him. For a second, I think we might just keep going, but he finally lifts his head and gives us an indulgent look. "Breakfast. Now."

"Yes, Sir." I make a half-hearted salute with one hand.

Derek laughs and hauls me up with him. We go our separate ways long enough for me to pull on my robe and the guys to grab their lounge pants. I stop in front of the windows in the living room. Snow falls so thick, I can't see the trees that were so prominent in the view yesterday. Or the mountains. Or anything but white. White that's building up against the glass. I frown at it. That has to be at least a foot of snow and it's showing no signs of stopping. "Um."

"Yeah." Grayson doesn't look over as he goes about dishing up three plates. "I called down to the lodge while you were occupied. The storm came in fast and is expected to linger in the area for another day at least. They won't be able to clear the roads until it passes, and it might be longer to get to the farther cabins like ours."

I blink. "Our flight is tomorrow."

"Doesn't look like we have a snowball's chance in hell of making it." He doesn't seem the least bit upset by this. Neither of us have work until after the New Year, but we had planned on spending the next week winding down and taking care of some projects that we had been putting off forever. Painting the living room. Finally go through the stuff in storage so we can donate what we don't want and keep the few irreplaceable things. Not to mention I was looking forward to a week of just us. Life can get so busy, it's easy to become ships passing in the night. I mean, we're hardly at that point, but it happened to my parents and I work hard to ensure it doesn't happen to me and Grayson, too.

That said...

I look at Derek. He's grabbed a plate from Grayson and eats, very pointedly not looking at either of us. If we're *forced* to stay here... "I guess we're snowed in."

CHAPTER 11

"*D*efinitely snowed in." Grayson sets my plate at the little dining room table across from Derek. I slide into the seat and he presses a quick kiss to my temple before retrieving his plate and taking the seat at the head of the table. We eat in silence, and for the life of me I can't tell if it's comfortable or tense. Maybe I'm the only one tense.

It was going to be difficult enough to move forward and pretend things with Derek hadn't changed if we went back to our normal life at the end of the twenty-four hours. Were we supposed to do it while still in this cabin, with memories of our fucking imprinted on every room in this house? Well, it wasn't yet, but give us a little time. I'm sure we'll make the rounds.

I look over at Grayson and he seems entirely too pleased with himself for him to be contemplating the end of this arrangement. "What are you thinking, husband?"

"No reason to stop as long as we're here." He very carefully doesn't look at Derek. "As long as everyone is in agreement."

Derek stays focused on his food. "I'm in."

"I am, too," I say slowly. There's no point in speaking my misgivings. They're not about the extended time. I'm worried that we're never going to want to stop. Except is that a problem? We already spend an inordinate amount of time with Derek. What if we…

I push the thought away. Later. I'll think about it later. Better to live in this moment right now and ride it as long as we can. I finish eating and take my plate to the sink. I turn around and nearly run into Grayson. He leans around me to set his plate in the sink, too, but doesn't move back. "You're thinking very hard, wife."

"Of course I am." I wrap my arms around his waist and hug him close. "It's what I do."

He presses a kiss to my temple and holds me close. "We have things under control."

"I know."

We're both lying, but it doesn't matter. I don't want to stop, and obviously neither does he. I don't know what life looks like on the other side of this, but we're not there yet. We get to live in the fantasy awhile longer. And if we're not finished with each other once the snow is cleared and we're on our way to the airport, maybe then I'll have the courage to bring up the messy thoughts tangling in the back of my mind.

I give Grayson a squeeze, enjoying the familiarity of the way his body fits to mine. "You know…" I tilt my head up enough to kiss his neck. "We haven't had a chance to try out the hot tub yet."

He releases me with a laugh and gives my ass a playful swat. "Go put on a suit and meet us out there."

I pout a little. "But what if I don't want to wear a suit?"

His expression goes heated. "Play along, Emma. I promise you'll enjoy it."

I'm already nodding. "Good thing I packed my new one

for this trip." Over the years my bikinis have gotten smaller and smaller. One of those things that I refuse to think too hard about, especially since I bought them right before our holiday trips. Grayson never commented on it, but he also loves taking them off with his teeth.

I pause by the nook table where Derek still sits. It's barely a choice to walk to him. More like a compulsion. I wrap my arms around him from behind and kiss his cheek. "Want to know a secret?"

"Always," he rumbles.

I press my breasts to his back and whisper in his ear. "I was thinking of you when I bought my suit this year."

He catches my hands, holding me against him. "You're playing with fire, baby."

"Oh yeah?"

"Yeah." He runs his hands up my arms, but releases me before we get anywhere interesting. I almost push him, but ultimately decide that the swimsuit will do the heavy lifting for me.

It takes a few minutes to brush my teeth, fasten my hair up in an artfully messy bun, and pull on the swimsuit. It's... scandalous is a good word. It's not quite a thong, but the back is cut high and narrow, leaving most of my ass exposed. The front triangle barely covers my pussy. The top is just as tiny, leaving my breasts looking like one wrong move could expose me.

And it's white. The second it gets wet, I might as well be naked.

I am, most assuredly, an asshole, but to be fair, I didn't *honestly* think we'd end up in the hot tub while we were here. Or if we did, I'd just wait for Derek to leave before I showed Grayson exactly how see-through my suit became. What can I say? I love tempting my husband into reckless fucking where we might be caught at any moment.

Being the reason Grayson loses control is like a drug to me. I am constantly teasing him when we're on dates, seeing how far I can nudge him until he drags me somewhere semi-private and we have our way with each other.

I half hope to find Grayson and Derek making out when I get out to the hot tub, but they're sitting on opposite sides, chatting about a mutual acquaintance. It's such a sheer shot of normalcy, it's almost enough to make me doubt what we've spent the last twelve hours doing. Or at least it is until they look at me with identical heat in their eyes.

Grayson raises his brows. "I think you left the rest of your swimsuit in the room."

I run my hands down my bare sides. "You don't like it?" I turn slowly, giving them plenty of time to ogle my ass. "I mean, I can go change if you really need me to."

Grayson shakes his head. "Get your ass in here."

I climb carefully into the hot tub and sink down next to Grayson. He's obviously got a particular way he wants to play this, so I'm content to follow his lead. Except he just keeps chatting with Derek. It's strange and so normal, all at the same time, and I settle down to relax in the warm water. The snow hasn't stopped falling, and it peppers my exposed skin with cool kisses, offsetting the heat permeating my body below the surface of the water.

"Emma."

I open my eyes and look at my husband. "Mmm?"

His brows lower, and my stomach gives a delicious little kick. I *love* it when he gets firm with me. "That suit is fucking ridiculous."

"I think it's sexy."

"No shit." He moves fast, grabbing me around the waist and towing me over to him. I end up kneeling on the seat next to him, which raises my upper half out of the water. Grayson glares at my breasts. "Baby, I can see your nipples."

"Whoops?"

"Don't even pretend like you're sorry." His gaze follows the water dripping down my skin. The cold kicks in almost immediately, pebbling my nipples against the thin fabric of my suit and raising goosebumps across my exposed skin. Grayson's still glaring at the water. "I bet if you stand up, I can see your pussy through those tease of bottoms."

"Maybe." I can't help smiling a little.

He turns to Derek, who's watching us with a closed expression on his face as if he's not sure how Grayson's going to play this either. My husband doesn't make us wait long. He looks at his best friend and then looks at me. "You wore this suit for him."

True guilt flickers through me because I *did* consider what Derek might do think if he saw me in this suit. "No, I bought it for you."

"Don't lie to me, Emma." He skates a hand up my spine and wraps his fist around my bun. One tug has me bending back against his arm. "You want him to look? He's going to fucking *look*." His voice snaps. "Get over here, Derek. Look at what my little slut of a wife put on for you."

The water moves slightly as Derek shifts closer. "Emma likes to put on a show. No harm, no foul."

"Your hard cock says otherwise." He tugs my hair again. It doesn't hurt. In fact, the sensation has me fighting back a moan. Grayson cups one of my breasts with his free hand. "I've seen the way you look at her, too, Derek. The way you're looking at her right now." He rubs his thumb over my nipple through the swimsuit. "If I wasn't here, you'd have your mouth all over her."

"She's your wife, man." He's not exactly protesting, falling easily into the roles Grayson has us playing. Except they aren't really roles, are they? The best friend and the wife. The wife and the best friend. That's what we are. That's all we're supposed to be.

"My wife wants to flash her pussy at you." He moves, hauling me up to sit on the edge of the hot tub and spreading my legs. Grayson runs his hand up my thigh and drags his thumb down the little triangle covering me. The one where we can all clearly see the shadow of my slit. "Fuck, she's not even pretending it's not true."

"Grayson—"

He gives me a forbidding look. "Not another word out of you." He pulls me back into the hot tub and nudges me back into the seat I originally occupied. "Sit there and think about what you've done."

"What have I done?"

His lifts his brows. "You've got Derek so turned on, he can't think straight. And *my* cock is hard and in need of fucking, but I'm hardly going to reward you for bad behavior. Am I, Emma?"

I clench my thighs together. "No?"

"That's right. No." He jerks his chin at me. "Hands on the side of the hot tub. You manage to be good until we're finished and I'll let Derek play with you."

I'm already nodding. "I can be good. I promise."

"Evidence suggests otherwise." He waits for me to put my hands where he could see them and then turns to Derek. They look at each other for a long moment, and then both seem to move at once. They meet in the middle of the hot tub, crashing together hard enough to send a wave of water splashing me. Grayson digs his hands into Derek's hair as he takes his mouth and Derek's hand is already moving below the water, obviously wrapped around my husband's cock.

Oh god.

I cross my legs hard, but it does nothing to relent the heat building inside me. If I could just touch myself...But I promised to be good.

To be good while they make out, their chests rubbing on each other, their hands moving below the water. I can't fucking *see* and it is both agony and a decadent tease. Derek pulls back and urges Grayson up, until my husband stands before him, his cock right at face level. He looks magnificent, water dripping down his fit body and his cock hard and long. Derek doesn't hesitate. He takes Grayson into his mouth and sucks him down, down, down, until his lips meet his hilt.

I moan. I can't help it.

Grayson looks at me as he digs his hands into Derek's hair. "I'm going to fuck you now."

Derek makes a sound of asset and then my husband is moving, fucking his best friend's mouth in long, brutal strokes. He looks fearsome and sexy as hell and I might come just from watching them alone. My body is one coiled line of tension, begging for some kind of release. It's so, so good and so bad, all at the same time. Derek takes everything he gives, the bliss on his rugged face just as sexy as the glare on Grayson's. It goes on and on and on, until I'm whimpering and writhing along with them. When Grayson finally comes, he does it with a rough curse, pumping into Derek's mouth as Derek swallows him down.

They break apart, all three of us breathing hard. Grayson sinks back down to his seat and waves a lazy hand in my direction. "Help yourself, Derek. I'd say you earned it."

CHAPTER 12

erek doesn't hesitate. He grabs me around the waist and lifts me, turning so I straddle him. He kisses my breasts, starting on the bared curves and working his way to where my swimsuit is already cold against my skin. Maybe that's why his tongue feels so devastatingly hot when he sucks my nipples through the wet fabric. I dig my hands into his hair and arch my back. "More."

Derek grips my ass with his big hands, pulling me down against his hard cock. And then his mouth is on mine. I taste the saltiness of Grayson on his tongue and that makes me moan as much as the feeling of Derek's hard length pressing against me.

He lifts me up to set me on the edge of the hot tub next to Grayson and then delves a hand between my thighs, dipping beneath my suit to stroke me. "She's so fucking wet, Grayson."

"Keep the suit on." My husband watches us with hot eyes. "That's the rule."

"Mmm." Derek moves back enough that I get a good look at him. I don't know why him being wet makes him even sexier than normal, but it does. His thick body glistens with droplets of water that I want to lick off. He doesn't give me a chance. Instead, he fists his massive cock and rubs it over my pussy. "Tug your suit to the side, baby. Let me see that pussy you keep teasing us with."

Grayson snorts. "Hardly keeping with the spirit of the agreement."

I'm already moving to obey, spreading my thighs wider and tugging my suit to the side. It doesn't matter that it's still snowing, that it's cold as fuck outside, because I feel like I'm burning up. Derek doesn't seem to have an issue, either. Not as he holds Grayson's gaze and eases his cock inside me. When my husband doesn't protest, he grabs my hips and yanks me onto his length. I catch myself on the edge of the hot tub but it's Derek's strength that holds me up as he begins to fuck me. If I let go, we'll both end up under water, so I'm helpless to do anything but take each thrust. To hold perfectly still as he nuzzles my top aside and lavishes attention on first one breast and the other, all while his cock is impossibly deep inside me.

"You're not even pretending you're not fucking my wife right in front of me." Grayson shakes his head, feigning disappointment.

"Sorry. Fuck, sorry." Derek pulls out of me and turns me around, moving me as easily as if I was a doll. Then he's inside me again from behind. He moves us back to his seat and sits down with me still impaled on his cock. "I'll stop fucking her." He readjusts my top, though he doesn't stop playing with my breasts. It doesn't matter that Grayson just saw him shove his cock inside me. We're playing a game again, a game of *we shouldn't*.

We pretend we're all sitting here, having a normal conversation, even if my sitting in Derek's lap is hardly normal. We pretend that we're being good. Being *just friends*.

We certainly pretend that Derek hasn't wedged his giant cock into me while my husband sits a few feet away.

"Don't move." Derek murmurs in my ear. "You wouldn't want him to know I'm still balls deep in your tight little pussy, would you?" He bands on arm around my waist, sealing us together tightly. "If he finds out what we're doing, we have to stop, and you don't want to stop, do you, Emma? You want me to keep fucking you slow and subtle. He'll never have to know."

If anything, Grayson's brow inches higher. "Everything okay, Emma? You look a little flushed."

I lick my lips. I search for words, but Derek chooses that moment to thrust up into me, ever so slightly. "I'm good," I moan.

"Baby, you're a terrible liar." Derek's barely speaking above a whisper. His free hand slides down my stomach to stroke my clit. "You better get your game face on or he's going to realize you're about to come all over my cock. What a little slut you are, Emma. Fucking me while your husband is *right there*." Even though he's speaking softly, there's no way Grayson can't hear. From how intensely he stares at us, like he might slip his leash at any moment, he can hear perfectly.

I feel like I'm melting. I cup my breasts, playing with my nipples even as Derek keeps up that slow stroking of my clit. I was already close before we started. Now I feel like I might die from pleasure. I try to shift my hips, but Derek keeps us sealed together. I huff a breath. "I'm just trying to get comfortable."

"Sure you are, baby." Derek keeps stroking my clit. "You're not shifting because your greedy pussy needs to be fucked hard. I can't give it to you. Not right now. Not with him watching." He does another of those tiny thrusts. "You'll have to be happy with this. It'll have to be enough."

"Don't stop," I whisper.

He doesn't. He keeps fucking me in those tiny thrusts that nevertheless send little ripples away from our bodies to where Grayson sits. My husband turns to look out over our view. "It's a good thing it's snowing so hard."

"What?"

"It'd be a shame if our vacation neighbors saw what a little slut my wife was. Trying to pretend she's not riding my best friend's cock right in front of me." He tsks. "Derek take off that tease of a suit and fuck her properly. Now."

Derek practically rips the top off me. He unties the bottoms and tosses them to join my top on the floor with a wet plop.

I don't know why losing the suit suddenly makes me feel a thousand times more exposed. All I know is that I need to fuck Derek and I need it now. "Please."

Derek loosens his grip enough that I can start riding him. Fucking in a hot tub is honestly less than ideal, but I can't seem to bring myself to care. Not when it feels so dirty to have Grayson watching my breasts rise and fall out of the water with each stroke. He narrows his eyes. "Up."

I barely comprehend the order, but Derek is already obeying, lifting me and rising to sit on the edge of the tub. I wince at the slap of cold air, but he's already urging me to keep sliding up and down his cock. I lean back against him and look at my husband. "I'm sorry."

"No, you're not." He crosses to us, his face level with where Derek's cock spreads my pussy. Grayson runs his hands up my thighs. "No, you're not," he repeats. And then his mouth is on my pussy. I watch him lick my clit and then Derek lifts me enough that Grayson can get to the base of his cock, which he gives the same treatment with his mouth.

"Oh my god."

"Come on his cock like a good little slut." Grayson

reaches between Derek's thighs and I know without a shadow of a doubt that he's cupping his best friend's balls, that he's stroking his perineum. "Better hurry before I make *him* come." And then his mouth is on me again.

I stop trying to ride Derek's. Instead, I dig my fingers into my husband's hair and grind down on Derek's cock. "Oh *fuck.*"

Derek cups my breasts even as kisses that spot on my neck that drives me crazy. "I love how much you love watching my cock in your wife's pussy, Grayson. Almost as much as I love sucking *your* cock." He lowers his voice. "Do you think you can give this up, Emma? Or do you think that the next time we're alone you're going to be rubbing that pretty pussy all over me?"

Grayson laughs against my clit. "As if you won't have your hand up her skirt the second you get a chance. Have her sit in your lap the way you are now and pretend like you don't have your cock inside her. Pretend like she's not taking you deep while we chat." He looks up at me. "Hopefully, you can last longer than you did today, baby. Or will you give up all pretense and ride him right in front of me?"

I come. I can't help it. No matter how much I want to hold out, to keep this going on forever, my body has other ideas. I barely finish the last wave when Derek pulls me off his cock and I watch Grayson suck him down. Derek curses as he orgasms, and my husband swallows him while holding my gaze.

I'm not a particularly religious person, but this feels like heaven.

We end up back in the hot tub, letting the heat soak into our bodies once more. My bones have gone all melty and I curl up in the seat of the hot tub while Derek and Grayson pick up their conversation easily.

This is what it could be like.

I close my eyes and finally let the thought settle in. This thing with Derek doesn't feel like a normal fantasy game I play with Grayson. It hasn't from the start. He's not a stranger we picked up at the bar, though that's one line we haven't crossed because Grayson decided long ago that it's not safe enough. He's not some person who's a stand-in for our lusts, who will walk out the door at the end of this, never to be seen again. He's our *friend*.

Derek's words from earlier echo through my head. Even if he and Grayson never consummated their attraction until now, they are more than friends. They've always been more than friends. They've always wanted each other, even if the timing was never quite right. They've always loved each other.

What if the timing is right now?

I try to look at it from all angles, but I'm tired and the men's easy conversation soothes me until it's hard to focus. I don't know how it would work for us to try. I don't know if all the relationships would survive the attempt. I honestly don't know much beyond a single truth: it will hurt all three of us to walk out of this cabin and pretend we never crossed these lines.

CHAPTER 13

"*E*mma." Grayson's voice has a fondness that suggests he's said my name a few times. I open my eyes just as he catches my hand and tugs me up. "Let's go inside."

I'm so distracted by my thoughts, I barely register what we're doing until Grayson leads me into our bathroom and turns on the shower. I glance back at the door and frown. "Derek?"

"He's going to take a shower in his bathroom and join us after."

"He's running."

Grayson lifts his brows. "Emma, we have this until the snow clears. It's okay for him to take a shower alone."

I search his face. He's always been good at hiding his emotions when he needs to, but it's been a very, very long time since he's tried to hide them from me. He's locked down right now. Completely closed up. I walk to him and slide my arms around his waist, hugging him tightly. "I don't like thinking about the end, either."

Grayson sighs and wraps his arms around me. "You're too damn observant."

"Hard not to be when I'm feeling something similar." I give him a squeeze. "You don't have to hide how you feel, not from me."

"You're my wife."

I already know where he's going with this. "And you're my husband. But that doesn't change the fact that we both care about Derek."

Grayson frames my face with his hands. "You are first for me, Emma. Always. I meant every word of those vows when we were married, and I mean them now."

"I did, too," I whisper. Now's the time to speak up, to tell him what I want just like I have every other time before in our relationship. "Grayson…" I take a deep breath and shore up my courage. "We've never had what most people call a conventional marriage."

He searches my face. "There are limits."

"Why?"

"What?"

"Why should there be limits? If it's what we want—what we *all* want—then why not do it? We don't give a shit what other people think now. Do you honestly think that's going to change in the future?"

He slowly shakes his head. "It's about more than us. Don't you think Derek deserves someone who will put him first? To be more than just a third to a couple wanting to play with kinky shit?"

"Grayson." I narrow my eyes. "You have never shied away from what you want. Not once in all the time I've known you. Until now. Derek is a grown man. He can make his own decisions just like we can. But don't you dare cheapen what we've shared this Christmas. He's our friend. He's…Well, I think it's pretty obvious he's more than that to both of us."

He tenses against me, and I brace for an argument, but Grayson finally sighs. "He is my best friend, Emma."

"Yes, I'm aware."

"Even if we were fully onboard, he'd never go for it." For my husband to admit as much means he's thought about it, too.

I take his hands and lead him into the shower. "But what if he did?"

His eyes are still filled with all the complicated emotions in my chest, but he smiles down at me. "You say that like you have a plan."

"Calling it a plan is exceedingly overstating things." Now it's my turn to hesitate. "I love you, Grayson. So much that sometimes it feels like my heart will shatter ribs and burst right out of my chest." I take a slow breath. "But doesn't it feel like something's clicked into place with Derek? Like the three of us just *fit?*"

He ducks under the spray for a long moment. When he wipes water from his face, all the complicated mess is gone, replaced by resolution. "Yes." He searches my face. "You're sure?"

"As sure as anyone can be in this situation." I try for a smile. "You were right in the hot tub, even if we were playing games then. It's going to be impossible to be around him without slipping up. The connection is too strong." I hesitate. "I think it's too strong for all of us."

His smile turns wry. "I suspect you're right." He glances at the door. "Derek might not go for it."

"Grayson, you're underestimating your charm. You know better." I grab soap and start lathering up my body. "It's simple enough to get the conversation started. We seduce him."

He barks out a laugh. "Baby, you're a gift."

"That's precisely what got us into this to begin with." I grin at him. No matter what else happens, Grayson and I are solid. This won't change that truth. I believe that down to my very soul. But I also meant what I said. We could be more. Not because we're deficient in some area, but because Derek adds something we didn't even realize we needed. He's already been playing that part to some extent by nature of our friendship. I want him to play it in our bed and home and future, too. But it can't just be me pushing this.

I sober. "If you don't want this…"

"I do," he says it on a sigh. "Fuck, but I do want this." He looks down at me with those gorgeous blue eyes. "Does that make me a selfish man, Emma? To want you and want him, too?"

"Probably." I smile. "But then it makes me a selfish woman, too. I want to have my Grayson and eat my Derek, too."

He gifts me with another of those free laughs. "I love you."

"I love you, too."

We don't speak again as we finish washing off and step out of the shower. I take the time to dry my hair and pull on my silk robe. Grayson waits for me, and if I didn't know better, I'd think he was nervous. Hell, if I didn't know better, I'd think *I'm* nervous, too.

We walk out into the main room to find Derek has built up the fire again. The snow continues to come down steadily, and I'm glad of it despite the headache it's going to be to deal with flights and the like. Speaking of… "We should probably call the airline."

"I'll take care of it." Grayson heads for his phone, pauses to kiss Derek on the temple, and then retreats back into our bedroom. If he sees the thunderstruck look on his friend's face, he doesn't stick around long enough to react to it.

I walk into the kitchen and Derek slides his arms around me seeming without thought, his gaze on the door my husband just closed. "Hey," I murmur.

"Hey." He finally looks down at me. "You look happy."

89

"I am." I smile. "I don't know about you, but this has been the best fucking Christmas—pun entirely intended."

Derek laughs. "I'm not even going to try to argue that. I don't know how you'll top it next year." His hazel eyes shutter, though he makes an obvious effort to keep his smile. "A printed tie isn't going to cut it."

"Oh, I don't know about that." I slide my hands up his thick stomach and chest. "Especially if I tied you to our bed with it and Grayson and I have our wicked way with you."

"Emma."

I ignore the warning in his voice. "Grayson's probably going to be busy for a bit."

"Uh huh." He motions at the kitchen. "It's been a hot minute since breakfast. We could use the calories."

"Oh, definitely. Calories. Yep." I hook my hands into the top of his lounge pants. "I'm starving."

"Emma."

"Derek." I mimic his serious tone and give him a sweet smile. "I haven't had your cock in my mouth yet and I'm dying for it. After I suck you off, you can feed me."

His brows draw together. "How am I supposed to argue with that?"

"Easy answer: you're not." I tug on his waistband, towing him out of the kitchen and into the living room. I pause. "The question you should be asking is whether you want me to give you a blow job, or whether you want to fuck my mouth."

He rumbles out a laugh and walks over to sit on the couch. "Wanting me to do all the work. Greedy."

"Always." I sink between his big thighs and he lifts his hips enough for me to free his cock. Derek's been on his knees so often for me in the last day. It feels right to have our positions reversed, to be the one doing the seducing, even if he doesn't realize that's my aim. I wrap a fist around his cock and lick my lips.

If someone asked me a week ago if I loved Derek, I would have answered that of course I do. He's Grayson's best friend, and he's my friend, too. Of course I love him.

In my heart of hearts, I knew it wasn't as uncomplicated as that, even before this Christmas. As I look up into his roughly handsome face, I feel the words bubbling up in my throat. Words that he's obviously not ready to hear. Words guaranteed to make him run, snowstorm or no. I can't say them. Not now. Not until we've played out our seduction and made the case for turning our couple into a throuple.

I swallow the words down. I swallow Derek's cock down, too.

He sifts his fingers through my hair and pulls it back from my face. If I thought about it, I'd have put on some red lipstick, but there's something pleasing about this. No artifice, not really. Just us. I take my time, enjoying myself as I explore him. The reminder that we're not in a rush makes it hotter this time. I can play with him until we both are ready to explode.

Derek gives my hair a tug. He's breathing hard already, his eyes glazed as they watch his cock disappear into my mouth. "Fuck, Emma. You love this as much as I do, don't you?"

I hum my assent and stroke my hands over his thighs. He's so *big*. It makes me shake with need and I don't bother to resist snaking my hand between my thighs to stroke my clit. This holiday has made me oversexed and I'm going to be sore for a fucking week, but I don't care. It's worth it. It's more than worth it. If this ends when the snowstorm does, I want to know I didn't miss a moment of it.

"You're stroking that greedy little clit, aren't you?" He

exhales and leans back against the couch. "Get up here, Emma."

I ignore him and keep sucking his cock. Derek looks at me as if he can't decide whether to drag me up his body or let me finish him off. I make the decision for him, reaching between his thighs to cup his balls. I give him a squeeze and just like that, his fingers tighten in my hair and he's thrusting up into my mouth.

There you are.

I relax instantly, letting him drive this, trusting him. It's a little rough and a whole lot sexy, and when he comes, I drink him down without hesitation.

Derek hauls me up into his lap and kisses me. He wraps his arms around me and I feel so fucking safe, I'm suddenly sure I can stay like this forever. I clamp my mouth shut to keep myself from saying something that will ruin this moment. He's been as all over the place as Grayson and I have been, and if we've settled on an endgame we'd like, I don't know if Derek has.

I don't know what we'll do if his endgame doesn't match ours.

He rests his chin on my head. "Merry Christmas."

"A very merry Christmas." I snuggle closer. "Grayson mentioned that you're cutting down on travel." Derek's spent most of the time I've known him bouncing from city to city for jobs, staying long enough to see his design put into reality before he moves on. He keeps a home in New York, but he only comes back for a few months at a time in between projects.

"Yeah, I got an offer at a local company. It's a different set of responsibilities, but the pay is good and it means I only have to travel if shit goes sideways with a project."

My heart leaps and I lift my head. "So you'll be around more?"

"*Around* is relative since you two moved out to Brooklyn."

I snort. "It's a train ride away." But even as I say it, I know I'm a liar. Yes, it's only one train ride, rather than a flight or something like that, but it might as well be a different city for all Derek is going to make the regular trek from Manhattan.

Unless we give him reason to.

CHAPTER 14

After we eat lunch, Derek has to take his turn wrangling the airline, and then we all end up on the couch watching a movie. It's some artsy type of thing that both Derek and Grayson are into, and I end up falling asleep against Derek's side. I must move at some point, because when I wake up, I'm lying on the couch with my head on his thigh, his hand heavy on my hip.

I blink my eyes open to find him and Grayson making out again, and I bite my lip because I know beyond a shadow of a doubt that this will never get old. My shifting must clue them in on the fact that I'm awake because Derek reaches down to cup my pussy without missing a beat. He spears me with two fingers even as Grayson delves his hands into Derek's pants and starts jacking him. I reach up and grab his wrist. "It's time."

It's a token of how well we know each other that no further explanation is needed. Without another word, we take ourselves to our bedroom.

I pause in the doorway, a flutter of nerves alighting in my stomach. I know what comes next, and I want it more than anything, but what if we fuck it up and ruin things with Derek? I look at Grayson, but for once he doesn't anticipate me. He's too focused on Derek. My husband considers him. "We're both going to fuck you."

Derek gives a faint grin. "Sure." For all his attempt at smiling, his shoulders are tight and he seems almost jumpy. As if maybe, like me, he just realized that this is a new step past the point of no return. And, just like that, my nerves fall away. I want to make Derek feel good, to make him feel valued.

To make him feel loved.

I cross the few steps between us and slide my hands up his chest to loop around his neck. "Hey."

He exhales slowly and catches my hips. "Hey."

"You don't have to do anything you don't want to do."

His lips quirk into a small, but very real smile. "It has nothing to do with not wanting to, and everything to do with after."

After this is over.

I open my mouth to ask if there needs to be an *after*, but Grayson cuts in before the words can emerge. He grasps the backs of both our necks and kisses first me and then Derek. Then he urges us to kiss.

How many times has Derek's mouth been on mine in the last twenty-four hours? More than a few. This kiss feels different. It's harsh and desperate and I sink into it even as I feel Grayson take my robe off and then move around to slide down Derek's pants.

Derek backs me up to the bed and we tumble onto the mattress in a mass of questing hands and needy bodies. And still we don't stop kissing. I let the worries about *after* slide away as he rolls onto his back and takes me with him, until I'm straddling his wide stomach.

Distantly, I can hear Grayson walking into the bathroom,

but Derek grips my ass and rocks me against his stomach and I can't focus. I moan against his mouth and try to get closer.

The mattress dips as my husband joins us, moving to kneel behind me. His lips coast a path down my spine, and he nips my ass before his touch disappears and Derek jerks. I know even without looking that Grayson has his mouth around Derek's cock. As tempting as it is to sit up and look back so I can watch, this is a seduction. If things go well, I'll have countless opportunities of watching these two men together. For now, I'll have to be a little less greedy.

Except it doesn't *feel* less greedy as I writhe in Derek's strong arms. It feels like heaven.

Grayson grabs my hips and pulls me back. It breaks the contact of our kiss and I whimper in protest. My husband hooks me around the waist and urges me up until my back presses to his chest. Grayson cups my breasts and Derek arches up to capture first one nipple and then the other. I'm bracketed in by these two and I've never felt safer than I do in this moment.

"Are you feeling needy, wife?" Grayson shifts one hand to grip Derek's hair, holding his face against my breasts. "Are you craving Derek's big cock in your pretty pussy?"

"Yes," I gasp. "Please."

"And you, Derek?" His voice goes lower and rougher. "Are you feeling empty, too?"

Derek lifts his head and looks over my shoulder to meet Grayson's gaze. "Fuck yes."

"Good." My husband urges me back a little more and then reaches down to wrap a fist around Derek's cock. He guides the other man into me and, fuck, this feels like a whole different level. I don't even know *why*. It's no more filthy than anything else we've already done. It doesn't seem to matter what should be, only what is.

I have to work myself down Derek's cock, but eventually I seal us together. That's when Grayson leans around and grabs a pillow. "Up, Derek."

Derek lifts his hips and I have to plant my hands on his stomach to keep my balance as Grayson wedges the pillow below him. I understand why the second I look back and watch my husband adjust his grip on the bottle of lube in his hand. He meets my gaze and lifts his brows. "Need something?"

"This angle is terrible for watching you fuck his ass."

Grayson laughs and gives my hip a squeeze. "Next time. Now be a good girl and ride his cock."

I am hardly ever a good girl, but his words light a fire inside me. I turn back to find Derek watching me closely. There's something in his eyes, something soft and warm that feels like a hook in my chest. I reach down and take his hands, lacing our fingers together, and guide them up to either side of his head. The new position leaves me entirely pressed against him and it's the most natural thing in the world to kiss him again.

I can *feel* the moment Grayson starts working his cock into Derek's ass. The man beneath me goes tense for one long moment and then sighs against my mouth and relaxes completely. His hands clench mine, a firm reminder that I'm not actually pinning him at all. That he's allowing this. I move on his cock in agonizingly slow strokes, wanting this moment to last. Needing it to last.

Grayson grips my hip with one hand, an anchor of sorts to keep me from floating away completely. Pleasure builds in slow waves, our breathing and the soft sounds of fucking filling the room.

Then my husband grabs my shoulder and pulls me up until he's once against pressed against my back. The difference is that he's fucking Derek this time. Grayson strokes his hands down my sides and then over Derek's stomach. "He feels good, doesn't he, wife?"

"Yes," I moan.

Grayson's voice goes deeper yet. "He feels like ours."

Derek looks up at us, and this time there's no denying that his heart is in his eyes. He looks at us like we're a feast he'll never be able to partake in. Like we're something distant instead of right here with him. He grasps my hips. "Don't say shit like that."

"Even if I mean it?" Grayson thrusts hard, lifting both Derek and me a few inches. We all moan in response. Too good. Is it possible for a thing to be too good? Surely it can't last.

Except I want to find out if it can.

Derek doesn't answer, and it's just as well. We devolve into beasts, fucking mindlessly. He thrusts up into me with every stroke Grayson makes, gripping my hips so tightly, I suspect I'll have a constellation of bruises from his fingertips. I relish the pinpricks of pain, relish the knowledge that I'll be carrying around a little physical memory from this moment. Grayson snakes a hand around my waist and down to stroke my clit. Always seeing to my needs, even while balls deep in Derek.

I come apart with a cry. Grayson bears me down to Derek's chest and then he's kissing him as Derek releases inside me. Grayson pulls out a bare second before he comes in great spurts across my ass.

We lay there panting for several long moments. The room seems to be doing a lazy spin around me, but Derek's chest is wonderfully solid beneath my cheek.

Grayson gives us another minute before he hauls all three of us into the bathroom and we take turns in the shower. Through it all, a strange sort of tension rises. We've had easy silences before, more than I can begin to count.

This isn't that.

Worry rakes hot claws through my stomach as I towel dry my hair. They *still* haven't said anything. Even though I know better—sometimes when Grayson is working through a particularly complex problem at work he needs time and space alone—I blurt, "Would someone *please* say something?"

"Nothing to say." Derek finishing drying off and hangs up his towel. Without another word, he walks out of the bathroom. I listen to his footsteps cross our bedroom, the soft sound of him pulling on his pants, and the door shutting softly behind him.

I turn to look at my husband. "What was *that?*"

Grayson wraps his towel around his waist. "He's putting distance between us."

"No, shit. *Why?*"

He scrubs a hand over his face. "It hurts too much to do anything else. Derek lives by the rule that it's better to leave before people leave him. I don't think he's been dumped once in the time I've known him. Maybe his first girlfriend, though I couldn't say for sure."

I frown. "We're not going to let him get away with that."

"Emma, give the man some space."

That's what Grayson has done over the years. Over and over again, and I suspect that's why they never sealed the deal before now. Well, that's not how I operate. I step to him and press a quick kiss to his lips. "I'm going to go get him."

"Emma," Grayson warns.

I walk out of the bathroom and peek out the window. "It looks like the snow has stopped. We don't have much time."

"Baby, some things aren't meant to be."

I know him well enough to recognize the undertones of fear in his voice. My husband is just as fucking terrified as Derek seems to be. I understand, though I don't have the history of quite as much baggage as they bring to this. Maybe that's for the best. Maybe it means I can see things clearest of us all.

I cup Grayson's face in my hands. "You love him."

"Emma—"

I kiss him again. "It's okay. Give me some time to talk to Derek and let's see what I can do."

"Talk, huh?" Some humor creeps into his tone.

I smile a little. "Sometimes talking and fucking go hand in hand, husband. You know that. It's how you snagged me."

"That's the damn truth." He sighs. "Okay. You're probably right. I'm not... I'm not thinking clearly right now."

I give him one last kiss. "I love you."

"I love you, too."

After some quick consideration, I pull on my silk robe and walk to Derek's bedroom. The door is unlocked, which is all the invitation I need to turn the knob and step inside. The room is identical to ours, positioned to maximize the view of the mountains with a giant king sized bed and large bathroom. Derek sits on the edge of the bed, his head in his hands. He barely looks up as I shut the door and lean against it. "I need some space."

"It's not going to do you any good."

That makes him actually *look* at me. "Easy for you to say."

"It's really not." I walk to him, stopping a few inches shy of his knees. He's tall enough—or I'm short enough—that our positions put his head nearly in line with my chest. But he's not ogling my breasts right now. He's staring up at me as if I contain the answers he's afraid to ask for.

Because I do.

But Grayson's right; I can't come at this head on. If Derek is feeling skittish enough to flee when the glow has barely worn off from some of the hottest sex I've ever had in my life, then he's likely to jump out the window and start hiking down to the lodge if I press him now.

Seduction.
What we need is seduction.

CHAPTER 15

I smile. "Did you like sleeping with us last night, Derek?"

His gaze shutters, but he finally huffs out a breath. "No shit, I did. Even if you snore."

That pulls me up short. "What?"

"Oh yeah." He grins. "It's cute though. Kind of soft and snuffling like a little pig."

I prop my hands on my hips. "Now I *know* you're fucking with me."

"Guilty." He reaches out almost hesitantly and clasps my waist. "It's Grayson who snores."

"Only a little." I let him guide me closer, until I have to hitch a leg up onto the mattress and straddle him. The move parts my robe a little, until it's barely being held in place by the tie.

Derek looks down and gives a long exhale. "This doesn't feel real."

"I don't feel real to you?" I settle against him and slip my arms around his neck. It brings us nearly chest to chest, but I let him keep that little bit of distance. Let him choose.

"Fuck, Emma. You feel real as hell." His hands shift on my hips, fisting the fabric a little as if he can't quite help himself. Derek watches his movements part it more, until my breasts are entirely bared. "This was a mistake."

Words I desperately don't want to hear. I don't move. I barely breathe. "It doesn't have to be."

"How can it be anything but that?" He moves one hand to cup my right breast, stroking his thumb over my nipple. "A glimpse of paradise before the gates are shut."

"That's rather poetic of you, Derek."

"What can I say? I see you naked and I get inspired."

I laugh a little even as I fight not to moan. His hand at my waist dips beneath the fabric to press against my skin. I don't understand how we've spent an entire twenty-four hour period getting lost in each other and he still affects me like this. Except I do. Grayson and I are years into our relationship and I still get twisted up over him. This feels the same and yet different. Like a puzzle piece we didn't even know we were missing and now that it's slid into place, our puzzle will forever be incomplete if he leaves.

"Derek…"

He kisses me before I can find the words. It's deep and unhurried, a slow exploration of each other. Almost as if kissing for the first time. Almost like he's saying goodbye.

No. Not goodbye. Not until we've at least had a chance to try.

I dig my hands into his hair and tilt his face back, pressing myself tighter to him as if the feel of skin against skin will be enough to keep him tethered to us. It's not enough. Not for me. Apparently not for Derek, either.

He slides his hands down my sides, opening the robe completely, and grips my ass. For once, this isn't about role-playing or pretending we're in a different situation. It's just us. Just a growing desperation to cling to what little time we have left. I want it to be more. God, I want it so bad, I can barely think about it because it hurts too much. But if that's not in the cards, if we have to go back to pretending we didn't share this glorious Christmas unlike any other… Well, I'm greedy. I want every last memory to hold close when missing him gets too bad.

Derek lifts me, rising off the bed so he can kick off his pants, and then turning to lay me down on mattress. He hits his knees at the edge of the bed and yanks me closer. "I'm going to dream about your pussy for years, baby." He drags his mouth up my thigh. "Every time I see you in one of those tight little skirts, I'm going to think about this moment, when I could do anything I wanted to you and you'd beg for more."

"Yes." I dig my fingers into his hair and try to guide him to my clit. I know I'm supposed to be the seducer in this scenario, that I'm supposed to be making a case for the three of us to be together, but I'm addicted to the way Derek eats my pussy.

But he resists my urging, moving to my other thigh and kissing my sensitive skin there. "Tell me what you need, Emma."

"I need you." My body is one tight line. I can feel each of his exhales against my pussy, but he's too strong for me to do more than let him drive this. The knowledge thrills me. "I'm always going to need you, Derek."

He nips me right at the top of my thigh. For a second, I think he might actually respond, but he moves up and drags his tongue over my pussy. I moan even as I try to focus. "We should talk."

"We'll talk later," he murmurs against my skin.

"Derek, I'm serious." I start to sit up, but he stops me with a hand on my stomach. A thrill goes through me at the thought that he could simply hold me down and eat my pussy until he got tired of it, and there isn't a single thing I could do to stop him. Just hold me down and make me come again and again until I stop being able to form words.

That's one way to end an argument.

"Derek," I gasp. He thrusts his tongue into me and then moves up to slide it against my clit. Even as I tell myself to focus, I can't help rocking my hips as much as I'm able, riding his mouth. It feels good. So freaking good. "Derek, *please*."

He moves faster than he has right to, shoving to his feet and flipping me onto my stomach. He drags me off the edge of the mattress, barely giving me a chance to touch down on the floor before his cock is inside me. Derek leans down and brackets my shoulders with his hands, covering me with his body even as he starts fucking me in long, rough strokes. "Please, *what*, Emma? Please make you come again and again and again like the precious little slut you are? Please betray everything I care about because I'm obsessed with your pussy? Please don't drag you somewhere nice and private the next time I see you and fuck you with my tongue before sending you back to your husband?"

I fist my hands in the comforter, moaning and writhing and completely unable to form a coherent argument. "Not just that."

"Not just that." He grips my hips and yanks me back as he thrusts forward, shoving his cock impossibly deep inside me. "Legs up on the bed."

I awkwardly obey, bringing my knees up to perch on the mattress. Derek shoves my thighs as wide as they can go and maintain this position with my ass in the air. Then he starts fucking me again, rubbing his cock against a spot inside me that has my entire body morphing into something liquid and hot. No longer flesh and blood and bones; I am pure lust. Pure love. "Oh *fuck*."

He slows down, doing something with his hips that

nearly makes me black out. "You didn't answer my question, Emma." Again and again and again, he rubs on that spot. "Please *what?*"

"Stay," I cry out. "Be ours. Fuck me whenever you want, however you want."

He thrusts deep and presses his body hard to mine, pinning me to the bed. Derek's lips brush my ear. "You say that when I'm fucking you hard and dirty, but the second we get back to real life, you'll start questioning it. You'll change your mind."

"No."

"Yes." He grinds into me, stealing my breath. "You might last long enough to make sure my addiction to your pussy, to Grayson's cock, really sets in. And then you'll go back to your happy marriage to each other and I'll be left in the cold."

I shove back, and Derek hesitates, but finally pulls out and lets me turn around. I waste no time pulling him back to me, guiding his cock back inside me. I wrap my legs around his thick waist, trying to hold him in every I'm able, and look up into his hazel eyes. "You're wrong."

"I'm not."

"Yes. You are." I kiss him hard, but some things need to be spoken aloud. "Derek—"

He uncrosses my legs and rolls onto his back, taking me with him. I blink down at him for a moment, and he gives an unexpected grin. "Ride my cock, Emma. Let me watch you fuck me. It's the least you can do while you're breaking my heart."

"I don't want to break your heart," I whisper. "Neither of us do. We just want you."

"It will never work."

That wasn't a no. I press my hands to his thighs, arching my back, and begin riding his cock. "But what if it does?

What if you get me like this whenever you want me? What if you can fuck Grayson whenever you get to feeling needy?" I bite my bottom lip. "What if we get all the sexy moments and all the soft moments and just *all* the fucking moments, Derek? What then?"

His gaze is glued to where his cock enters me. I keep fucking him, waiting for a response, but apparently I'm not going to get one. Not now. That's okay. I like spinning out this fantasy that could be our reality if we'd just get out of our own way. "Don't you like how I fuck you, Derek?"

"Yes," he growls.

"Don't you want this always?"

He grabs my hips. "Fuck. *Yes*, Emma. Is that what you want to hear? I want this pretty little fantasy you're spinning where I get you and I get him and it somehow works. But that's not real life."

I press myself to his chest and kiss the corner of his mouth. "Not real life? Is it fantasy that your best friend's wife is fucking you right now with his enthusiastic approval? Is it fantasy that if you come back to our bed tonight, you'll fuck Grayson? Is it fantasy that I love you?" Shit. Shit, I didn't mean to say the last out loud.

Derek goes perfectly still beneath me. "What?"

"I think you heard me."

"You love me." He sounds almost shocked. "That's bullshit. You just love the feeling of coming around my cock."

That's about enough of that. I use my hands on his chest to rise up so I can meet his gaze. "Yes. And all the various ways of fucking we've done over the last twenty-four hours. But don't you dare cheapen our friendship by saying I don't love you, you asshole. You don't get to tell me how I feel."

"Emma," He looks downright tormented. "You're not making this easy."

Because he doesn't feel the same way.

I swallow down my hurt, shove it down deep. It's not comfortable, but I have to respect what he's saying. I have to *try*, at least. I attempt a smile. "You're right. We're talking too much." I pull myself off his cock and move up his chest. "Eat my pussy, Derek. If we only have until the snow clears, I want as many memories of this as I can store up."

He does. He eats me out until we're both covered in sweat and I've come more times than I can count. Until I beg him to stop because I can't take another lick.

Only then does Derek agree to come back and go to bed with us.

We walk back to my bedroom naked, Derek's giant cock so hard that it looks like it hurts. I almost offer to take care of it for him, but I suspect Grayson will have his own ideas about it. I'm not so greedy to deny my husband that, especially not when this is apparently goodbye. One last hurrah because Derek doesn't believe we can make a go of this. I'm not sure I blame him. What are the odds we could make it work? Unconventional doesn't begin to cover it. We might have a chance with all three of us onboard, but if he doesn't have faith in the outcome, we're doomed before we start.

No one says a word, but what would be the point? Grayson takes one look at my face and understanding dawns. He gives me a small smile, a promise of reassurance, and then focuses on Derek and his giant cock. "Get over here."

They meet at the edge of the bed, a clashing that's almost violent. Derek topples him back to the mattress, and their hands are everywhere. Stroking and gripping and attempting to pull each other closer.

My chest feels tight just watching them. This could have been our life. If we'd realized what we wanted earlier. If Derek was open to the idea. If we hadn't fucked this up. If, if, if.

They thrust together, but it's not enough. By the time Derek looks up, I already have the bottle of lube in my hand. I pass it over silently, and he motions to a spot on the mattress next to them. "Come here, Emma."

I sink down and lean against the headboard. My body is still zinging from everything Derek did to me in his bedroom, but my desire ramps up at the sight of him spreading my husband's legs and sliding his lubed up cock into Grayson's ass. "Holy shit," I breathe. It was sexy as hell to be in the middle of the ménage, but watching them fuck is just as hot.

It's not the pure mechanics of it, though seeing them strain toward each other with every stroke is a sight to behold. No, it's the way Grayson looks up at Derek. He doesn't have to say that he loves his best friend. It's right there for both of us to see. Just like it's blatantly obvious that he's saying goodbye the same way Derek is saying goodbye.

It makes me want to scream. I have to close my eyes and breathe through it, have to let go of my hurt over the rejection. We're the ones that changed the rules. Not Derek. It's not his fault that we couldn't keep to the terms of this Christmas gift.

I open my eyes in time to see Derek orgasm, grinding into Grayson just shy of brutally. He barely pauses before sliding down my husband's body and sucking his cock. Through it all, he has eyes only for Grayson. I can't read his expression, can't tell if it's regret or love or something else altogether in his eyes.

Grayson reaches over and laces his fingers through mine. He's still gripping me when he comes, pumping into Derek's mouth as his best friend swallows him down.

Fuck, that's hot.

Once everyone recovers enough to move, we end up back in the bathroom. I finish first and take the opportunity to switch out the sheets with the spare ones in the closet. By the time I've remade the bed, they're still not out and I start back toward the bathroom door only to stop short when I hear their low voices.

I should turn around, should go to the kitchen and pour myself a giant glass of wine. Or some water. Something, anything, but moving closer to the bathroom door to eavesdrop. But then, I never was that good at anything resembling self-control. I lean against the wall next to the cracked door and listen.

"Why not?" That's Grayson, his frustration evident in his voice.

"It's easy for you to ask that." Derek speaks softly, almost as if it pains him. "You have nothing to lose in this little game. You still have the perfect wife, the perfect fucking life. If this blows up in our faces, that won't change."

"If this blows up in our faces, I lose *you*. I hardly think that counts as nothing."

Derek's breath hitches. "Stop saying shit like that."

"No. We've danced around this since college. You are my best friend and I love you, but I want you, Derek. I've wanted you since college. Tell me that the last couple days don't feel like a missing piece sliding into place. Tell me this wasn't fucking perfect."

"It wasn't fucking perfect."

Grayson gives a bitter laugh. "Great. Now tell me without lying."

"It won't work. Whatever you two are picturing of a life with me, It won't work."

"How do you know if we don't try?"

It doesn't matter how compelling Grayson's argument is. Derek has already decided. It was clear back in his bedroom with me, and it's clear in his silence to my husband's question. I don't get a chance to figure out if I should interrupt.

Derek stalks out of the bathroom, through the bedroom, and out the door. He never once looks back.

I slump against the wall as Grayson steps into the bedroom. He looks as tired as I feel, but he tries to give me a smile. "I tried, Emma."

"I know." I step into his arms and give him a tight hug. "I'm sorry."

"Me, too." He hesitates and finally exhales, long and slow. "Baby, I know you love him."

"He rejected us."

"Yes. *Us*." He moves back enough to meet my gaze. "Consider this Christmas present without a finish date."

I frown. "What are you saying?"

"I'm saying even if there aren't the three of us together, I'm not going to keep you from him." He must see the panic fluttering through me because he quickly adds. "I'm not letting you go, baby. You're my wife and I love you. Nothing that's happened this weekend has changed that." He smooths my hair back from my face. "I'm just saying that Derek has bedroom privileges for as long as you want him to."

Three days ago, the offer might have thrilled me. Now, it feels like a sad silver medal when we could have had gold. "Did you tell him this?"

"No. It's up to you whether you want to do anything about it." He gives me a pained smile. "There's no reason we should both go without." Grayson hesitates for the barest amount. "Before you ask; it's not just about you. I don't want him to be alone, Emma. He won't accept shit from me going forward, but he will from you."

"That's not fair," I whisper.

"Life isn't fair." Grayson glances at the door. "You should—"

"No."

"No?"

I shake my head. "He made his thoughts very clear about what we're offering. I'm not going to go crawling back to him for a second time tonight." I go up onto my toes and press a light kiss to my husband's lips. "Let's go to bed. We'll talk more in the morning."

CHAPTER 16

*T*he morning dawns with skies clear of clouds. It's beautiful and makes my chest ache for what it means.

Our holiday is over.

So is our Christmas fling with Derek.

It feels strange to stand in the kitchen and drink my coffee while the men make phone calls that will take us off this mountain and back to the real world. I have to hold perfectly still to contain my impulsive need to beg them to hang up and let us linger in this place a little while longer. It won't help. Derek's made up his mind about the future, and it's cruel to hold us in this purgatory any longer than necessary.

I don't know if Grayson told him about our conversation last night. I don't know if *I* want to tell him. It doesn't matter if Grayson gave permission, that he's lobbing me at his best friend in a last ditch effort to keep the precarious balance between the three of us; it feels like continuing to want Derek makes me a horrible wife. I love my husband desperately. I never want a life without him in it. But the last few

days have only stoked my desire for Derek—my love for him
—higher.

What a mess.

I escape to the bedroom to pack. Anything to dodge the
growing tension between the three of us, thick with things
left unsaid. Except that's not the problem, is it? We've said
everything there is to say and it's still not enough. Some
hurdles even love and sex and decent communication can't
overcome. That's just life. It sucks and I hate it, but there's
nothing I can do to change it.

I pull on a floral dress that buttons down the front and
am searching for a pair of fleece leggings when I hear footsteps behind me. I turn to find Derek standing in the doorway. He's wearing jeans and one of those flannel shirts that
make him look like a sexy lumberjack.

His gaze drags over me, starting at my bright red toes and
ending at my eyes. "Emma."

It's like his presence sucks the very air out of the room.
"Yes?"

He takes a step toward me, and then another. "I like the
dress."

"Thanks?" I shake my head slowly, trying to focus past the
desire that instantly surges in his presence. "Is that what you
came in here to say?"

He opens his mouth, seems to reconsider, and gives a
rueful grin that sinks a hook right into my heart and tugs.
"We haven't left the cabin yet."

My body goes scorching hot. "We have to leave soon in
order to make the rescheduled flights."

"Grayson says we have an hour."

A small eternity and not nearly enough time at all. I know
what my husband is doing, recognize his method of paving
the way to the future he wants. If he can't have Derek, then
he figures me having Derek is the next best thing. I want to

yell, to shake Derek, to convince him that he's making a mistake by turning away from this without even trying. But if I push him, I might push him right out of our lives completely. It would hurt me. It would destroy Grayson.

So I don't say all the words bubbling up in my chest. I simply nod. "Then I suppose we better hurry."

Derek moves closer, leaving the door open behind him. "Unbutton that cute little dress, Emma. Let me see what I'm going to be missing."

Again, I almost tell him what Grayson and I talked about. Again, I hold back. I don't have to make a decision now. It's possible my husband made that offer and he'll regret it later. It's possible *I'll* regret it later if I take him up on it.

But Derek's right; we're still in the cabin, still within the parameters of our extended Christmas.

I slowly unbutton the front of my dress to my waist and then tug the fabric aside. Derek hisses out a breath. "No bra, Emma?" He moves closer yet, until he's almost touching me. "If I pull up your skirt, am I going to have your pussy bare, too?"

"Only one way to find out," I murmur.

He sinks to his knees in front of me. He's tall enough that his face is nearly level with my bared breasts in his position. I reach out and dig my fingers into his hair, pulling him closer until his mouth is on me. "I'll tell you a secret if you want."

"I want," he growls against the curve of my left breast.

"I never wear anything under my sundresses." I gasp as he pulls my nipple into his mouth, but force myself to keep talking. "Grayson loves to fuck me whenever the mood strikes and panties just get in the way. We fuck in the bathroom at parties, in the car on the way home." He moves to my other nipple and I moan and tighten my grip on his hair. "We fuck in your parking garage nearly every time we visit."

Derek moves down my body, kissing his way over my

stomach. "You walk into my apartment all filled with his come."

"Yes." I shiver. He nips my lower stomach but doesn't move from there. I take a slow breath. "It feels particularly dirty to be having a conversation with you while he drips down my thighs."

He presses his head to my stomach. "Fuck, Emma. What am I supposed to do with that?" He curses. "Every time I see you, I'm going to wonder if he's just been inside you."

"You could always check so you know for sure."

Derek doesn't hesitate. He runs his hands up my legs, barely pausing where the hem of my dress brushes my upper thighs before he shoves it up around my waist. He pushes me back onto the bed and spreads my thighs. One thorough lick later and he lifts his head. "I don't taste him on you."

"Then you have your answer, don't you?"

"Guess I do." He looks down at me, and I try to see myself from his perspective. My dress does a better job of framing my nakedness in our current position than covering anything. My skin is flushed and I'm breathing hard despite the fact that we've barely done anything. My entire body is shaking with a pure bolt of need. Derek strokes up my thighs and uses his thumbs to part my pussy. "Show me."

"What?"

"At some point, you're going to start remembering how good it felt to fuck me and you're going to touch yourself. Show me."

I don't hesitate to reach between my thighs and stroke my clit. He's kneeling next to the bed, getting a close up view of me masturbating, and the look on his face only makes this hotter. So I double down. "I'm going to think about how you ate my pussy on the couch that first time. You fucking *tricked* me, and then Grayson caught us and joined in and..." I moan.

"I always peek at my presents ahead of time." His breath

ghosts against my thighs. "Grayson knows that. He sent you to me on purpose."

I slow down my touch, wanting to make this last. "And then when we played out that fantasy on the couch. When I rubbed my pussy all over your cock and took you deep." I inhale sharply at the bite of pleasure. I have to be careful or I'm going to come and then it ends. "You felt incredible inside me, Derek. Your giant cock fills me so good."

His lips brush my knuckles and then his tongue is sliding between my fingers licking me. He winds me tighter and tighter…and then lifts his head. Derek looks almost angry as he shoves to his feet and his hands go to the fronts of his pants. "Your husband told me the damnedest thing just now."

I freeze, watching him draw out his cock. "Did he?"

"Yeah, he did." He grabs my hips and yanks me to the very edge of the mattress. "He told me to help myself to your pussy whenever I feel like it." Derek guides his cock into me in a rough thrust. Again and again, until I'm trying to clutch him closer. He takes my hands and pins me to the bed, fucking me hard and deep. "I know what you're doing."

I moan. "Let me touch you."

"No." He strokes deep and stays there. He's still wearing all his clothes, his jeans shoved down barely enough to get at me. I can feel the denim against my ass, his flannel rubbing my breasts with every shaky breath we take. Derek glares down at me. "You don't get to seduce me with your tight pussy, wet just for me, and your perfect fucking breasts and that mouth that likes to spin out dirty fantasies no good girl would admit to."

Just like that, I'm as angry as he is. I lean up and catch his bottom lip, biting down just hard enough to make him flinch. I lick the spot and sink back to the mattress. "You are choosing to walk away, Derek. Not me. Not Grayson." I unwrap my legs from his waist, not quite sure when I linked my ankles at the small of his back. "You like it when I play the little slut, and you'd fucking love it if I showed up at your apartment and told you not to tell my husband but I need your thick cock too much to go another night without it." I hold his gaze. "That's just pretend, and we both know it. Just like we both know that I'd go straight back to him and describe exactly how hard you made me come while he licked all evidence of you away."

He stares down at me. "He wouldn't."

"You damn well know he would." I yank my hands free and shove at his shoulders. He lets me roll us, ending up on his back with me still on his cock. I brace my hands on his chest and start riding him. "You're the one who wants to deny Grayson what he wants, Derek. Not me. Never me. And if what he wants is for me to fuck you, then that's what I'll do." I lean down until my lips brush his ear. His hands go to my ass, gripping me tightly as he guides my strokes. I let him have this because it feels good to be held by him, because I have more to say. "You could have both of us; morning, noon, and night. In every fantasy you've ever wanted to play out, in every position and place you can think of." My breath comes out in something resembling a sob. "Just like you could have the nights with Grayson cooking one of those fancy meals of his, and late nights reading with me, and lazy Sundays, and *all of it.*"

"Emma, stop."

I lean back and hold his gaze. "You are the one choosing not to, Derek. So forgive us if we're willing to take you however you'll let us."

He hooks my neck and pulls me down to meet his mouth. I know it's just to shut me up, but I don't care. I've said what I needed to say. It won't change anything, so I grab the pleasure he offers now with both hands. We devolve into grasping hands and moans and pure animal fucking. I come hard and Derek follows me over the edge, fucking up into me hard enough to extend my orgasm and have me shrieking. I collapse on his chest and turn my face toward the door.

Grayson stands there, his expression the pure agony of seeing something he desperately wants but no longer has access to. He spares me a brief smile that fails almost as soon as his lips curve and then he walks out of the room without looking back.

I don't know how to fix this. I don't know if it's possible, if I should even try.

So I simply press a kiss to Derek's lips and climb off him. I button up my dress without another word and duck into the bathroom to clean up as best as I can. I expect him gone when I return to the bedroom, but he's still sitting on the edge of the bed, his clothing now righted.

He watches me pull on my leggings, his expression just as tormented as Grayson's was early. "I don't want to lose either of you."

"Then we never should have crossed this line." I can see that now, even if I couldn't in the midst of Christmas Eve, with lust clogging my senses. We had no business going there unless we were willing to go the rest of the way. I *knew* it wasn't as simple as playing out a sexy fantasy, that Grayson wanted Derek even more than I did.

It's too late for regrets.

I grab a hair tie from my suitcase and pull my hair back into a ponytail. "*That* offer stands, Derek. Our door and our hearts are open to you." I glance at the doorway. "But I'm not going to hurt Grayson. He thinks he wants me to fuck you if he can't, but I won't do that to either of us. This is the last time."

"You said—"

"I know what I said." I give a mirthless smile. "You should know better than anyone things said in the heat of the moment are to spike the pleasure. I want you. I'm never going to *not* want you. But you only want to fuck me, and he's my husband. He isn't afraid to admit that he loves me."

His brows draw together. "That's not fair."

"I know." My throat feels tight. "Just… Just think about it, okay? Can you promise me that?"

He nods slowly. "I wish I could say I'm going to think about anything else for the foreseeable future."

CHAPTER 17

Grayson and I barely speak on the flight back to New York. The silence isn't exactly fraught, but it's a sign of things changing. Things I desperately don't want to change. I manage to make it until we're back in our apartment before I burst. "Are you mad?"

My husband looks at me with something akin to shock. "What? No. Not even a little bit." He pulls me into his arms and wraps me up tight. "I'm sad. It feels like we opened Pandora's box on Christmas Eve, and it's going to take time to put things back into their place."

I press my face to his chest and breathe in his clean scent. "What if we can't?"

"Then we go on differently than before." He strokes my hair and presses a kiss to my temple. "Let's unpack and I'll order in some Thai. You pick a movie tonight."

"Okay," I whisper. It's a blatant olive branch in the middle of something that isn't really a fight, but that doesn't change the feeling of the ground shifting beneath my feet. "We're okay, right?"

"Yeah, baby. We're more than okay."

But as the days pass, I start to worry that we're both lying about our level of okayness. It's nothing overt. We spend the remaining days between arriving home and New Year's Eve like we'd planned; painting the living room, but skipping organizing the storage.

I'm a bit superstitious about getting life in order during the week between Christmas and New Year's Eve. I believe that how a person enters into the new year makes a difference. It's why we are always fucking when the clock strikes twelve, why I go a little planner crazy with things I want to make sure happen in the next twelve months. Grayson has indulged me since we started dating, and this year is no different.

Except it *is* different.

It feels like we're missing part of us, like we left it back in Colorado in that cabin with Derek. There's nothing *wrong* with Grayson and I, but I keep looking over like I expect Derek to magically appear. And when Grayson and I have sex, it's pure fucking. He drives my pleasure like if we can just orgasm enough times, we can purge this feeling of *missing* away. I don't know if it works for him, but every time I stir on the other side of coming, the memories of those few days crash over me in waves.

It's not just missing the sex with Derek, though. Interspersed in those memories are ones from farther back. We've spent so much time together over the years, and it never really occurred to me that we could be a throuple instead of a married couple and Derek playing the comfortable third wheel. But we *fit*. Every piece of evidence points to us fitting.

It's a damn shame Derek doesn't agree with us.

New Year's Eve feels more bittersweet than any year past. Grayson chats with me while I set up my new planner, putting on the designing show marathon on television and

122

referencing his digital calendar as we work through each month.

When we finally reach December, I stare at it. "Are we doing another trip with Derek for Christmas?" It wouldn't be a question I'd ask normally; our annual Christmas trip with Derek is tradition. It's a given. Until it's not.

"I don't know," Grayson says softly. "Mark it in pencil or washi or whatever temporary option you have."

My chest tries to close and I blink rapidly against the burning in my eyes. "I'm sorry."

"Baby, no." Instantly, he's up and around the table, bending down to cup my face. "I'm sorry it's hurting now, but I'm not sorry we did it."

"How can you say that? You're friendship with Derek is changed forever."

Grayson shrugs a little. "Friendships change. We'll figure it out once he's had time to think. I'll take him however I can get him, even if that means it's not what we wanted." He strokes my cheekbones with his thumbs. "Are *you* okay with that?"

"I'm not going to sleep with him again." I catch his frown and rush forward. "It doesn't feel right without you involved. And no matter what games I like to play, I already have feelings for Derek. Being confined to only sex will make me resent the hell out of him, and it's not worth it to add bad feelings to confusing ones."

He finally nods. "Okay. But my offer remains open if you change your mind." He glances at my planner. "I think we're good?"

"Yeah. We're good." For a moment, it even felt like it. No matter what else is true, Grayson and I will find a way forward through this. Our foundation is too strong for the outcome to be anything different. I wrap my hands around his wrists. "I didn't say this before, but if you want to be with him, I'm okay with it."

He goes perfectly still. "What?"

"If you want to keep having sex with Derek." I study his face. I didn't feel threatened at all when they were fucking with me nearby, and I can't ignore the sliver of doubt that tries to worm its way into my heart. They've known each other so much longer than Grayson and I have, have been nursing an attraction to each other in addition to their friendship. Sending Grayson into Derek's bed might be a mistake. But I want him happy, and if we can't have Derek in our bed and in our life in a permanent way, then this is something I can give Grayson. "I'm okay with it."

Grayson pulls me to my feet and kisses me hard. "Thank you for offering that, but I'm not going to take you up on it for the same reasons you won't."

"The offer stands, though."

He smiles down at me, the first real smile I've seen on his face since we left Colorado. "I love you, Emma."

"I love you, too." I go up on my toes to kiss him again.

The buzzer sounds.

We look at each other. "Did you order food all sneaky-like?"

He shakes his head. "I hadn't gotten around to it yet. I was waiting until you finished with the planning marathon."

The buzzer sounds again. I step back from Grayson, my heart doing something fluttering and worrisome. "Better see who it is." I have no business hoping. Absolutely *no* business letting that feeling blossom in my chest.

He presses the button to call down to the front door. "Yeah?"

"I'd like to talk."

The blood rushes out of my head at the sound of Derek's voice, even tinny from the speaker. He's here. I turn back to the table with my planners and start to put them to rights. Anything to keep my hands busy as Grayson buzzes him up. I can't believe this is happening. Except I don't know *what* is happening. He might be stopping by to tell us to our faces that he never wants to see us again. That we broke our friendship with him irrevocably when we crossed the line Christmas Eve.

By the time Grayson opens the door for Derek, I've got all my things picked up. It feels like a mistake because now I have nothing to do with my hands. I wrap my arms around myself and drink in the sight of him.

He looks good. Really, really good. He's trimmed his beard and he's wearing his customary jeans and T-shirt that's just fitted enough to show off his shoulders and chest and presses lightly to the curve of his stomach. He looks at Grayson and then at me, his expression carefully guarded. "I was hoping we could talk."

Grayson motions to the living room. "Sit."

Derek takes the chair. Grayson and I sink onto the couch across from him. My husband's hand finds mine, and I give him what I hope is a reassuring squeeze. The silence stretches out for several long beats, a tangled messy thing that none of us seem all that inclined to break.

Finally, Derek curses. "What would it even look like? If we went for this?"

The rushing in my head nearly drowns out Grayson's careful response. He's holding my hand tightly enough to hurt, but his body language is otherwise relaxed. Like he's afraid of spooking Derek. "We feel it out as we go. We keep communication open and talk to each other." A brief smile touches his lips. "We fuck."

Derek looks at me. "That's too simple. There's no way it'll be that easy."

Grayson takes a slow breath. "No one says it'll be easy. It

won't. Relationships can be challenging with two people, let alone three. But I'm willing to work through it in order not to lose what we started in Colorado. I can't promise that things won't be hard, but I can promise I'll work through whatever comes up."

"And if it blows up in our faces?"

That startles a ragged laugh from me. "Have you been enjoying the last few days since Christmas, Derek? Because we sure as hell haven't."

His eyes go soft. "No, Emma. I haven't enjoyed the last few days, either."

"We crossed too many lines to go back." I hate that it's true, but it *is* true. "The only way is forward. Can't we at least try? Would that be so bad?"

Derek scrubs his hands over his face. "What about the future? I want kids."

"So do we," I say slowly. I hadn't even considered how *that* would look, but the thought of raising kids with the three of us sends a jolt through me that's entirely too intoxicating. "Eventually."

Grayson snorts. "Probably sooner, rather than later."

"And what about events for work and all the shit that goes with raising a kid. You don't think people are going to notice that there are three of us?"

I shake my head slowly. "Derek."

"What?"

"Since when do you give a fuck what anyone else thinks? If we make it work, if we're happy, then the rest of the world can jump off a bridge for all I care. Our household is the only thing that matters."

His shoulders slump a little. "It won't be that simple."

"No, probably not." Grayson shrugs. "But we won't know until we try." He hesitates the briefest of moments. "Do you *want* to try?"

Derek leans forward and props his elbows on his thick thighs. "Yes. I want to try."

The air seems to rush out of the room. We stare at each other for a long moment before Derek continues. "I can't go back to being on the outside looking in. This wasn't the plan I had for my life, the partner and equivalent of white picket fence and kids and dog and all that shit. But if I haven't found someone who can compare to the two of you in the last eight years, I'm not going to be able to." He shakes his head. "No, that's a fucking copout. I don't *want* anyone but you two. I... love you both."

"Come here." Grayson's voice is rougher than normal.

Derek rises and walks around the coffee table. We part for him to sit between us, and it seems the most natural thing in the world to bracket him in and press against him from either side. I slip under his arm and cuddle close. "I love you, too."

"We both do," Grayson murmurs.

"This is a terrible idea. You know that, right?" Derek looks between us.

I laugh and give him a squeeze. "We'll find our way through."

We begin talking almost hesitantly, but settling into the conversation quickly. What it will look like for us to try. How we can adapt our lives to accommodate for three. If things go well, maybe Derek will move in with us before too long, though that will mean a larger apartment. Maybe a house with a yard and the full nine yards. Kids. *Kids.*

But all that is in the future.

My alarm goes off at eleven-thirty. Derek looks at me with surprise, but Grayson is grinning. He nudges his friend. "Emma's superstitious about New Year's Eve."

I push to my feet. "It's as much tradition as superstition and you know it." I hold out my hand to Derek. "I'm a firm believer in starting the year how you intend to move through it, and I want this year to be the three of us."

Derek snorts. "So *that's* what you two are doing at midnight every year."

"Guilty." Grayson stands. "And now it's the *three* of us."

CHAPTER 18

*W*e move into the bedroom and I light a few carefully placed candles while they undress. I turn in time for Derek to pull me into his arms as Grayson moves to press against my back. They undress me as quickly as they undressed each other, and then the three of us are pressed together, skin to skin. I want to hurry and I want to slow down, and the warring impulses nearly tear me in two.

Grayson twines his fingers through my hair and I eagerly give in to the slight pressure that guides me to my knees. I wrap a fist around Derek's cock and take him into my mouth. Was it really only six days ago that we had sex? It feels like forever. I suck him down, driven on by Grayson's hand in my hair, by Derek's soft curse.

I open my eyes to find them making out as I suck Derek's cock. I grip Grayson's cock with my free hand and move to suck him down. They allow me to switch back and forth a few times before Derek hauls me to my feet and takes the few steps to get us on the bed. He kisses me hard. "I missed you."

"I missed you, too."

KATEE ROBERT

Grayson presses against Derek's back and kisses his neck. "We don't have much time if Emma want us fucking by midnight."

I'm already nodding. "I do. I really, really do. We can go slow later."

Derek chuckles. "Always so ready to jump the gun. We have plenty of time." He moves down my body. I try to pull him back up, but he's so much stronger than I am. A thrill goes through me at how easily he ignores my tugging hands. I meet my husband's gaze as Derek drags his tongue over my pussy.

This is happening. He's here, really with us, really *choosing* us.

Grayson grins at me, looking happier than he has all week. He turns his attention to Derek. "Make her come. Then you can fuck her tight, wet pussy while I take your ass."

Derek growls his agreement against me. But he doesn't speed up. He takes his time reacquainting himself with my pussy, licking in thorough strokes that leave no part of me untouched. It's so, so good. I feel fucking *cherished*, and the way Grayson sifts his fingers through Derek's hair and guides him up to my clit only compounds the sensation.

This is real.

I try to hold out. I do. But the realization that I can have this whenever I want it, that this is the start of a new chapter in all our relationship... It pushes me over the edge as surely as Derek's wicked tongue does. *Mine*. These men are mine and I'm theirs and I've never felt more loved than I do in this moment.

Derek moves up my body and guides his cock into me. One inch at a time, sliding deeper by increments until we're sealed together. He frames my face with his big hands and looks down at me with his heart in his eyes. "I love you. I didn't say it before because I'm a fucking asshole, but it's the truth." He glances at Grayson as my husband approaches with a bottle of lube in his hand. "You already know I love you, but I'm saying it again now."

"I know." He sees the look on my face and bursts out laughing. "I'm kidding, Emma. You should appreciate the reference."

"Not right *now*."

Grayson sobers. "I love you too, Derek. Always have. This is just a new level of it."

I glance at the clock. "Hurry."

Derek thrusts into me, temporarily distracting me. "I like your superstitions, baby."

"You're about to get fucked by Grayson while you fuck me, so I just bet you do."

He chuckles against my neck, but the sound turns to a moan as Grayson moves behind him. I don't have to see clearly to know that he's working his way into Derek's ass. Then they begin to move, or maybe it's Grayson who's moving, his fucking causing Derek to fuck in turn. I don't know. It doesn't matter. The only thing that matters is how perfect this is. The weight of them keep me pinned to the bed, helpless to do anything but take what's given.

As the clock strikes twelve, Grayson reaches around Derek's hip and strokes my clit with his thumb. Slowly. Teasingly. Like he wants this moment of pleasure to last as long as possible before we lose control.

Somewhere in the distance a cheer goes up and there are fireworks, but they're nothing compared to what's happening right here, right now. I kiss Derek, giving myself over to the feeling of him filling me so perfectly, to Grayson's thumb moving in tandem with his strokes, working me closer and closer to orgasm.

It hits me between one heartbeat and the next, washing away every last bit of bad feeling that clung to me after this last week. None of it matters now. We're here. We're doing this. We're starting something new and wonderful and hope is a beautiful thing in my chest.

Derek follows me over the edge, driving into me and coming with a low curse that curls my toes. He slumps onto me, barely managing to get himself braced on his elbows to keep some of his weight off me. Not that I care. I want to be smothered with both of them right now. His body moves easily with Grayson's increasingly rough thrusts. It has me writhing around his softening cock despite my best efforts. "Oh fuck."

Grayson's laugh is strained. "Again, baby? You're so greedy." He doesn't stop stroking my clit, doesn't stop fucking Derek.

I don't know if I come again, or if it's just a second wave of the last orgasm. It doesn't matter. Grayson shudders and his grip on Derek's shoulder goes white-knuckled. I swear I actually hear him come on Derek's back. Grayson presses a kiss to his neck and eases back. "Don't move."

"Couldn't if I wanted to."

My husband disappears into our bathroom and returns a few moments later with a washcloth. He takes his time wiping up his mess and then smiles down at us. "Happy New Year."

"Happy New Year," I murmur.

Derek eases out of me and moves to my side. "Get rid of that and get back here. I have six days of missing out on you two to make up for."

Grayson's smile widens. "I am so fucking *happy* that you're here, Derek."

A few minutes later, we're all in bed together. It feels more perfect than I could have imagined. To be pressed between them, our hands wandering over each other's bodies, followed by mouths. Followed by more fucking.

We finally manage to get some sleep sometime before dawn. I open my eyes to the sunlight streaming in through the windows. We forgot to close the curtains.

Derek lays sprawled out on our bed, his hand wedged firmly between my thighs as if he couldn't resist touching me even in sleep. Grayson is pressed against his back, his shock of dark hair barely visible at the curve where Derek's wide shoulders meet his neck.

I don't know what the future holds. I know there will be challenges and difficulties just like there always are, but I have utter faith that we'll be able to see our way through. We have so much history of friendship with Derek, it almost feels like he's slipped seamlessly into our life.

Happiness bubbles up inside me and I scoot closer to Derek. Grayson's hand comes around his waist and strokes my hip. Yes. This is so incredibly perfect, only made more so by the knowledge that it doesn't end with the rising sun.

We can have this happiness, this joy, this *perfection*.

Forever.

* * *

THANK you so much for reading Grayson, Derek, and Emma's story! If you enjoyed it, please consider leaving a review.

WANTING MORE time with these three? Sign up for my newsletter to get access to bonus content for this book and all of my new releases!

LOOKING for a little more taboo in your life? Check out the first book in this series, Your Dad Will Do. When Lily catches her fiancé cheating on her, she decides to get revenge...by banging his dad. After this weekend, her ex won't be the only one calling his father Daddy.

KEEP READING to get a look at their story!

* * *

HOW DOES one go about seducing their almost-father-in-law? I really, truly do not recommend doing an internet search. The results are heavy on porn and light on answers. In the end, I'm left to my own devices.

That's how I end up on his front porch in a short black dress and thigh-highs in the middle of January, well after the polite hours of visiting. I'm shaking as I knock on the door, and it's not purely because the icy wind makes my clothing feel like a laughable barrier.

Despite the late hour, he's awake. My breath catches in my throat as the door opens to reveal him. Shane. The man who, up until a few days ago, was supposed to be my father-in-law. Funny how quickly things change when you least expect it. Or not so funny at all. I sure as hell don't feel like laughing.

He fills the doorway, a large man with broad shoulders, big hands, and a smattering of salt and pepper in his hair. He's in his late forties, some twenty-ish years older than me. Shane frowns as recognition slips over his handsome face. "Lily? What are you doing here?"

"I was hoping we could talk." I have to clench my jaw to keep my teeth from chattering. Maybe I should have gone with the trench coat route. At least then I'd have a coat.

To his credit, Shane doesn't make me wait. He moves out of the way and holds the door open so I can walk past him.

The first blast of warmth makes me shiver again. Maybe if I hadn't stood out there for so long, gathering my courage, I wouldn't be so cold now.

"What did he do?"

I blink and stop trying to rub feeling back into my fingertips. "Excuse me?"

"My asshole son. What's he done now?" He catches my hand and lifts it between us. My ring finger is markedly empty. Shane skates his thumb across the bare skin, still frowning. Now my shivers have very little to do with temperature and everything to do with desire.

It's yet another indication of the many ways that my relationship with Max wasn't operating on all cylinders. His freaking father can do more with a single swipe of his thumb than Max was ever interested in doing with his entire body. Then again, Max and I only ever had polite, friendly sex—which was *not* what I found him doing with his secretary when I showed up unexpectedly at his office. It's not what I suspect he was doing with the others I suspect came before her.

I don't want to get into it right now. I've already had four days of tears and raging with my girlfriends, but if I start talking about how I found Max fucking his secretary like the biggest goddamn cliché in existence, I'm going to start crying again.

That's not why I'm here.

I'm here for revenge—and maybe a little pleasure, too, though the pleasure rates a distant second in priorities.

"Shane." I say his name slowly. In all the time I dated Max, I called him Mr. Alby. A necessary distance between us, a reminder of what he was to me—only ever my boyfriend's father. I rip down that distance now and stare up at him, letting him see the pent up emotions I've spent two long years ignoring and denying.

I've spent two long years ignoring a whole lot.

Shane's dark eyes go wide and then hot before he shutters his response, locking himself up tight. But, almost as if he can't resist, he swipes the pad of his thumb over my bare ring finger again. "Tell me what happened."

"We're over." My voice catches, and I hate that it catches. "No going back, no crossing Go, no collecting two hundred dollars. Really, really over."

He nods slowly and then gives my hand a squeeze. "Sounds like you could use a drink."

"I could use about ten, but one's a good place to start." At least he isn't kicking me out. That's a good sign, right? I follow him to the kitchen and watch as he opens the liquor cabinet and picks through the bottles.

He barely glances at me. "Vodka, right?"

"Yes." Of course he remembers my drink. I bet, if pressed, he also remembers my birthday and a whole host of other details that slip past most people, including my ex.

But then, Shane isn't most people.

Heat melts into my bones as he methodically puts together a drink for each of us. I don't know what to do with my hands once I don't need them for warmth, and the coziness of the temperature is a vivid reminder of just how little I'm wearing. My dress is barely long enough to cover the tops of my thigh-highs and while I'm wearing a garter belt, I have nothing else on beneath the thin fabric of the dress. I'm dressed slutty and downright scandalous and Shane has barely looked at me since I walked through the door.

That won't do. That won't do at all.

He finishes with the drinks and I gather what's left of my courage and close the distance between us, sliding between him and the counter to reach for the glass. Just like that, he's at my back, his hips against my ass. "Thank you," I say over my shoulder.

He inhales sharply, but doesn't move back. "What are you doing, Lily?"

His lack of retreat gives me a little more strength. Just enough to sip the drink and then turn slowly to face him. I have to lean back over the counter to meet his gaze, and a thrill goes through me as he forces *me* to make the adjustments. He might as well be made from stone. I tip my chin up. "I have a question."

"Ask it."

"Last summer, you and Max were supposed to be working, so I was here at the pool." I can barely catch my breath. "No one was around so I didn't bother with a suit."

"Mmm." The barely banked heat in his gaze is back, flaring hotter by the second. He still hasn't moved, either to press against me or to retreat. "That's not a question."

I lick my lips. "It felt wicked to be out there naked, knowing I was in your house even if you weren't here. I…" This part's harder, but his nearness gives me a boost of bravado. "I started touching myself. I felt like such a little slut, but that made it hotter."

He's breathing harder now, and he reaches around me to grasp the counter on either side of my hips. "Why are you telling me this?"

"Because it's not anything you don't already know," I whisper. "You were upstairs. I saw you watch me through the master window." I reach behind me to the counter just inside his hands. The move arches my back and puts my breasts almost within touching distance of his chest. "I didn't know you were there when I started, but once I knew you were watching me, I took my time and dragged it out. I wanted you to watch. I wanted you to do more than watch." The last I've never admitted to myself, let alone out loud, but it's the truth. "Do you remember that?"

He exhales harshly. "You don't know what you saw."

"Okay." I'm shaking like a leaf. "My mistake."

Shane still doesn't move away. "Even if I came home for lunch unexpectedly that day, you were dating my son." He shifts forward the barest amount, closing in on me. "It would be fucked up if I stood in my master bedroom while you fingered that pretty little pussy. I'd be a monster to have watched the entire thing and fucked my hand while I pretended it was you."

"Shane," I say his name like a secret, just between us. "I'm not dating your son right now."

"What did he do?"

"I don't want to talk about it."

He shakes his head slowly. "You came here with a purpose, but you don't get to throw yourself at me without sharing the truth. Out with it, Lily. What did Max do?"

I really, really don't want to talk about it, but the sheer closeness of him makes my verbal brakes disappear. I find myself answering without having any intention of doing so. "He slept with his secretary. I think he wanted me to catch him. Either that, or he's just really shitty as hiding it when he's up to no good." Except that's not the full truth, but admitting that I think he's been cheating on me for months and months feels lke admitting that I'm a fool. What kind of fiancé just swallows the lies whole and doesn't question it when things don't quite line up?

Apparently the kind of fiancé that I am.

He curses softly. "I'm sorry."

"I'm not." It's even the truth. I will cry and I will grieve for the future I thought would be mine, and I sure as hell will spitefully fuck Max's dad, but I'm not sorry I avoided tying my life to someone who never should have been more than a friend. Someone who didn't hesitate to hurt me instead of sitting me down and telling me how unhappy he is. Max is selfish and if I wasn't entirely happy in our relationship either, I didn't go out and fuck other people when we were together.

But, as I told Shane just now, we're not together any longer.

I lift myself onto the counter, putting us at nearly the same height. The move has my skirt rising dangerously, flashing my thigh-highs and garters.

Shane looks down and goes still. We both hold our breath as he shifts one hand to bracket my thigh and traces the point where my garter connect with the stockings. "Lily." This time, when he says my name, he sounds different. Almost angry. "If I push up your skirt, and I going to find your bare pussy?"

The words lash me and I can't help shivering. I lick my lips again. "If you want to find out, I won't stop you."

"Dirty girl." He snaps the garter, the sting making me jump. "You came here for revenge."

There's no point in denying it. "Yes."

"I'd have to be a selfish asshole to take advantage of you when you're like this." But he's looking at me in the way I've always fantasized about, like he has a thousand things he wants to do to my body and hasn't decided where he wants to start.

"It's what we both want, isn't it?" When he doesn't immediately answer, I press. "Why *not* do it?"

He moves his hand to my hip and grips the fabric of my dress, pulling it tight against my body. "I could think of a few reasons. You were going to marry my son."

I can't quite catch my breath. "I'm not going to now."

"You're young enough to be my daughter."

I watch the dress inch up my legs with every pull of his hand, baring more and more of me. The sight makes me giddy. It's the only excuse for what slips out in response. "Should I call you Daddy, then?"

He goes still. Just like that, he releases my dress and the fabric falls back to cover most of my thighs. Disappointment sours my stomach, but he's not moving back. He skates his hand up my side barely brushing the curve of my breast before he grips my chin just tightly enough to hurt. "Is that what you want, Lily?" He presses two fingers to my bottom lip and I open for him. "You want to call me Daddy while I do filthy things to you that you've only fantasized about." He slips his fingers into my mouth, in and out, in and out, miming fucking. I watch him with wide eyes, but I don't get a chance to decide if I like it or not before he clamps his remaining fingers tightly around my chin, his fingers almost deep enough to gag me.

Shane leans down and holds my gaze as his fingers stroke my tongue. "You want to call me Daddy while I slip my hand up your skirt and find out what you have waiting for me? While I bend you over this counter and eat your cunt until you come?" It's almost too much, I can't quite catch my breath, I really *am* going to gag, but he gives me no relief. "You want to ride *Daddy's* cock?"

ONE-CLICK Your Dad Will Do now!

ACKNOWLEDGMENTS

Thank you to all the readers who've been just as invested in these taboo books as I have been. They're such fulfilling creative projects for me, so it makes me happy to know that they're giving you a little bit of joy in these challenging times.

Big thanks to Jenny Nordbak, Nisha Sharma, and Andie J Christopher for cheerleading this series and always shouting GO! MORE! when I'm considering dialing it back. You're right. You're always right.

All my love and thanks to Tim. Your support means everything to me. Love you like a love song!

ABOUT THE AUTHOR

Katee Robert is a *New York Times* and USA Today bestselling author of contemporary romance and romantic suspense. *Entertainment Weekly* calls her writing "unspeakably hot." Her books have sold over a million copies. She lives in the Pacific Northwest with her husband, children, a cat who thinks he's a dog, and two Great Danes who think they're lap dogs.

Website: www.kateerobert.com

Printed in Great Britain
by Amazon

46781998R00088